D0942660

How to Talk to Nice English Girls

by
Gretchen Evans

How to Talk to Nice English Girls © 2018 Gretchen Evans

ISBN 978-1-948272-09-4

All rights reserved.

Published 2018 by Carnation Books

CarnationBooks.com

contact@carnationbooks.com

San Jose, CA, USA

Cover design © 2018 Bran Heatherby of Crowglass Books

This book is a work of fiction. Any similarity to real persons, living or dead, is entirely coincidental and not intended by the author.

Acknowledgements

They say the family of the 21st century is made up of friends, not relatives. Thanks to my writing family for their love and support.

Contents

Chapter 1

Early March 1920

"Why is Mr. Fuller coming so early? I didn't know he'd be here at all," Cecilia hissed.

Marian pushed down the urge to hush her older sister. Cecilia was a grown woman, on the cusp of being married. She wasn't a child Marian could scold anymore. But the old habit still rose in Marian's throat.

"I didn't know either." Marian dropped her voice, hoping Cecilia would follow her lead. "I'm sure he isn't coming specifically for the wedding. Mr. Fuller must have business with Father."

Cecilia threw up her hands in dramatic fashion. "That's worse! Why would I want someone at my wedding who doesn't care to be there!"

Mr. Daniels, the Warwick Paddox House butler, gave a discreet cough behind them. Daniels was an older man, tall and whip-thin. All of his hair had deserted him long ago. Marian's eyes cut to him over Cecilia's shoulder. He was right, the foyer was not the place to speculate on, or, even worse, to disagree with their father's decree.

Marian pushed her sister gently toward the closed sitting room door. "Let's join Mama in the sitting room. There's nothing to be done about it, so we might as well have a nice evening."

Cecilia snorted but moved toward the sitting room. "Of course you think there's nothing to be done. You never do anything rebellious."

That stung, a bit. But it was true. Why would anyone want to be rebellious? That was asking for trouble. Best to stay quiet and reliable, to work around things as best you could.

Cecilia walked in front of Marian and the light glinted off her upswept pale blond hair and the delicate glass beads decorating the skirt of her evening dress. Cecilia was lithe and lovely and full of life. Marian's own evening dress itched against her skin and her corset felt too tight. She was drab and dull next to Cecilia.

Before Marian could follow her into the sitting room, Daniels cleared his throat. Cecilia didn't notice, but Marian turned at once.

"Lady Marian, your father would like to see you in the library."

Marian straightened her spine and redirected her steps. "Off to face the dragon," she muttered under her breath as she passed Daniels. He didn't laugh outright, he never did, but an eyebrow arched high on his forehead.

Marian suddenly felt rebellious, if that was what the jolt down her spine meant. Maybe she wasn't as boring as Cecilia thought.

The library was warmly lit. It smelled of leather and books and was deeply masculine in a way that appealed to Marian. It was one of her favourite places in the house. The women of the family had the run of it during the day, but by night William Fielding, Earl of Denbigh, preferred to take his evening port and cigar there.

From his desk, Lord Denbigh had an excellent view of the grounds through large floor to ceiling windows to his left. The desk was scattered with that morning's papers, advertisements for machinery, and business journals. He was a man that kept a close eye on all vantage points, both home and away.

Marian stepped directly in front of the desk. The need to stand directly in her father's line of sight was a lesson quickly learned in childhood. Even though she had been summoned, if she didn't make sure Lord Denbigh noticed her, she could easily go overlooked.

It took several minutes before he finally spoke, eyes still on one of the journals on the desk. "I know it was a shock to learn that Robert Fuller will be arriving for Cecilia's wedding. You're also smart enough to realise that this is a business necessity and not a social call."

The previous Earl had been one of the first of the peerage to embrace trade and investment as a means of securing his estate. The current Earl kept up and expanded the practice. But, times had changed. Landed families were running out of money, or out of heirs after the war, and estates were being sold all over the country. Lord Denbigh's investments and business deals were keeping them afloat, but Warwick Paddox House was not immune to this new economy.

Marian nodded.

"Mr. Fuller will also be bringing his daughter, Katherine. They arrive from New York tomorrow and will be staying with us for some time after Cecilia and Henry's wedding." He paused long enough to take a sip of port. "I am turning Katherine over to your care while they are in residence."

Marian should have expected something like this. Her father made demands, he did not ask favours. "In my care? Aren't they bringing their own governess?"

Lord Denbigh's attention turned fully to Marian for the first time. "Miss Fuller is nineteen years old. Robert lost his wife when the girl was a young child and she was allowed to run wild." The disgust in her father's voice at the word *wild* was obvious. "I believe she has already managed to alienate all good company in New York. I won't have her tendency for inappropriate behaviour reflecting badly on our family."

"So you're making me responsible for her?" Marian was at a loss for what to do with an uncouth 19-year-old girl for several weeks during the final preparations for Cecilia's wedding. Only her shock allowed her to question her father so directly. She was already busy handling household matters while her mother and Cecilia were preparing for the wedding. This would overwhelm her.

Lord Denbigh smoothed his hands across the papers covering the desk. "Marian, you are the most level-headed, appropriately behaved young woman I know." The corner of his mouth quirked up in the only version of a smile he used. "Certainly the more balanced and socially aware of my daughters. I trust you to be a good influence on her."

Marian smiled back. "Should I remind you that your daughters are the only young women you know particularly well?"

"Yes, and I will remind you that I never make a poorly planned decision." His concentration refocused on the financial section of The Times, which he had certainly read over breakfast. "Spend time with her, be a good influence, and keep her from doing anything that will disturb Cecilia's wedding or my business dealings."

Marian ticked off the list of preparations she would need to verify with the household staff before the Fullers arrived tomorrow. It wasn't an insurmountable task, but her work would only get more demanding as the wedding neared and as she had to give attention to Miss Fuller.

Lord Denbigh did not acknowledge her again and Marian knew she was dismissed. She slipped quietly from the room, but instead of joining the other women in the sitting room, she turned to the servants' stairs.

She went in search of Daniels. He had been with the Fielding family well before Marian was born. Daniels was an expert at balancing the harsh and sometimes unreasonable expectations of her father with her mother's flighty instructions. Growing up, Marian had learned much about negotiation and thoroughness at Daniels's knee. It was by silent agreement that she and Daniels had worked together to allow her to start taking over her mother's responsibilities with the household staff. Marian had been slowly moving into that role with her mother barely noticing.

She found him, shut away in his office beneath the stairs, counting the silver recently cleaned after dinner. He bent with aged and crooked back over his desk so that Marian couldn't see his face, only the barely-there wisps of white hair on the top of his head. Her soft knock brought him to his feet. He moved so much more slowly now than he had in her childhood.

Marian entered and sat in the chair opposite Daniels's desk. She waved him back to his seat and listened to his knees creak as he sat down. "Did you know that the Fullers were coming before Father announced it at dinner?"

Daniels regarded her over the rim of his wire frame reading glasses. "No, but I've had rooms in the East wing opened for them. The maids will finish their preparations tomorrow morning before the Fullers arrive. Their train is due in Warwick Paddox at ten o'clock in the morning and the car will bring them here promptly. A cold luncheon buffet has been ordered from the kitchen which will be laid out after their arrival."

Marian smiled. "I never doubted you, Daniels."

"Then why do I have the pleasure of your company, Lady Marian?"

Marian shifted in her chair. "Father wants me to take on Mr. Fuller's daughter." Daniels raised an eyebrow but didn't reply. Marian pushed on. "Miss Fuller is ill-mannered and Father has made it clear that I am to be responsible for her behaviour."

"She's American, but she can't be that bad, surely?"

"I honestly don't know. Father made it sound as if she's completely untamed. What am I to do with her?"

Daniels scoffed. "I certainly cannot tell you. Untamed young American girls are not within my professional knowledge. But I'm sure your excellent example will guide her in the right direction."

Marian rose from the chair, shaking off her moment of despondency. "Enough of that, then. Nothing to be done about it now, and since you've got this well in hand, I'll find somewhere else to be useful."

Marian made for the door but was stopped by Daniels's voice. "Your father could be right. If anyone I know can put wayward young girls back on track, it's you."

It was very hard for Marian not to stick her tongue out at him, as she might have done as a very young child. It was tempting to spite the idea that she was refined and matronly enough to train a woman only a few years younger than herself by acting childishly, but she tramped down the urge as she closed the door behind her.

Marian suddenly felt very weary. There was too much to do already, and now she had to keep Miss Fuller out of mischief. The beginning of a headache built behind her eyes as she thought of the consequences of failure for her family, for the estate itself, and for the people that had worked for so long below stairs. What would happen to them if Father failed to keep Warwick Paddox house afloat?

It was too much for Marian to think on tonight. In the morning she would meet Katherine Fuller and find out how difficult this task would be.

Chapter 2

Marian lay awake in the early morning hours, watching the still dark sky through the crack in her curtains. This was her favourite time of day: when the birds had just begun to sing and the sun rested behind the hills. She often stayed in bed, listening to the house rise for the day, until her lady's maid came to dress her.

The door creaked open and Marian stiffened her spine, the relaxing solitude of her morning falling away as she prepared herself to face the day. Her morning routine always made her feel like she was building a hard shell around part of herself so she could be who her family expected her to be.

"Good morning, Alice," Marian called out, her back to the door. Alice was early, judging by the weak morning light breaking through the curtains. Marian would have liked more time alone.

"It's not Alice. It's me."

Marian turned in her bed at her sister's voice. Cecilia, wearing nothing but a long nightdress, crept into the room, shutting the door behind her with a quiet click. Her bare feet shifted uncomfortably on the cold floor.

Marian threw back her covers and scooted back to make room. "What are you doing running around like that? Get in bed before you freeze."

Cecilia quickly tucked herself into bed, facing Marian. She slid her ice cold toes along the soles of Marian's feet. Marian twitched and pulled her feet back with a familiar sigh of exasperation. "Anyone would think you were the younger sister, going by the way you act. You are not as mature as a soon-to-be married woman should be."

"Do you think I'll suddenly grow older and wiser when Henry walks me from the church?" Cecilia laughed.

"No. I think you will both remain as foolish as you ever were." Marian smiled and laid her hand upon Cecilia's cheek.

She was genuinely happy for her sister. Nothing could diminish that. Henry and Cecilia were made for each other. They were happy together and married life would be kind to them. It was the best ladies like Cecilia and Marian could hope for. But there was a dark tinged edge to the happiness Marian felt for her older sister.

It wasn't jealousy, not exactly. More a sense of loss and an emptiness that gnawed at her. Cecilia and Henry had loved each other from childhood. They both had been bright and mischievous growing up. They were obviously drawn to each other from the start. Both Cecilia and Henry craved adventure and excitement in a way Marian had never understood. Cecilia had had a wonderful debut season in London before the war. Henry had watched, most often smirking from the sidelines, but confident in the knowledge that Cecilia would come back to him.

The Great War came and Henry went looking for his own adventure. He was sent home with a minor wound before the end and a new realisation that adventures aren't always safe. The number of young men who wouldn't come home at all made the slightness of Henry's injury seem like a blessing. Since his return to Warwick Paddox, he and Cecilia had been as inseparable as they were in childhood.

Marian had never had another person like that. Never had a person that seemed to fit with her the way Henry fit with Cecilia. Her own seasons had been uneventful and many of the young men she had known hadn't been as lucky as Henry. Marian had resigned herself to a life alone. She had never really wanted to marry, not the way Cecilia did, so this petty jealousy made even less sense. She missed a future she didn't even want.

"I am the happiest I have ever been, even more joyful than when Henry first stepped off the steamer from France. It's been months since he asked me to marry him and I am still happy." Cecilia's joy made her completely unaware of any hardship or ill will that might come her way. It only made her look lovelier too. Even at dawn, with scant hours of sleep behind her, the apple of Cecilia's cheeks was rosy, her deep blue eyes shone, and her pale blonde hair caught the rising light.

"You should be happy. Henry loves you very much."

Cecilia rolled on her back, taking a portion of Marian's blankets with her, and stared at the ceiling. "I never thought he'd ask so soon after getting back. I didn't think Father would agree to such a short engagement."

Marian chose her next words carefully. "I think the war changed a lot of people's expectations of how time flows. Shorter periods of time now feel like forever because it can all be taken away so quickly. People have stopped waiting."

Cecilia looked away from the ceiling and caught Marian's eye. "I think you're right. The young men who came back are different now."

I don't mean only the young men, Marian thought but held her tongue. Instead, she changed the topic to avoid discussing how little her older sister had changed during their times of hardship. As society itself was changing around them, Cecilia remained untouched. "What does Mama have you doing today to prepare for the deluge of guests who are about to rain down upon us?"

Cecilia rolled away with a huff. "We're going to town to see the dressmaker. I think Mama is just trying to keep me busy before the Fullers arrive. I let her know last night that I am not pleased that Father is using my wedding as an excuse to conduct business."

"You know he wouldn't if it wasn't necessary." Marian chewed her bottom lip. Everything she knew about the family's finances was derived from observation. Cecilia may not know anything at all. "Things aren't as they used to be. Many families have been in dire straits since the war."

That was the most Marian could bring herself to say. Even admitting that much caused a lump to rise in her throat at the thought of where they might be soon. Cecilia waved her away. "I'm sure everything is fine. It's always fine. Father just doesn't understand that now is not the time to discuss money."

Marian suddenly wondered, unkindly, how much Cecilia's wedding was costing.

"Did he really tell you to mind Miss Fuller?"

"He did. How did you know that?"

Cecilia rolled and stretched out on her back, dragging Marian's blanket down and letting cold air in. "Just gossip around the house. She has a reputation, you know."

Marian's stomach turned a bit queasy at the thought. "Father said she had acted inappropriately in New York."

Cecilia shook her head. "It's more than that."

"What is it then?" Marian's stomach flipped. She didn't know how to handle this situation as it was. She would be lost if Miss Fuller was truly scandalous.

Cecilia waved away her concerns. "Just gossip again." She turned her head to look Marian in the eye, expression much more serious than Marian was used to seeing. "I think it would be good for you if you liked her. You're always so lonely, Marian."

"I'm not lonely. I just have responsibilities to see to. I keep correspondence with both Elizabeth Cary and Marie Vesey." Marian was shocked. No one had called her lonely before. She wasn't lonely. She liked keeping her personal relationships simple. It made it easier for her to learn the role of the lady of the house, which she would end up doing in her mother's stead. This was her purpose, not to cultivate friendships or love that went nowhere.

Cecilia shrugged, all seriousness and concern gone. "All right. If you say so."

There was a soft knock at the door before Alice, the maid, entered. Cecilia rose from the bed, dragging all of Marian's blankets away. "Come on, up with you. It will be breakfast soon enough." With a wave, Cecilia was gone through the door, still only in her nightdress and with bare feet.

"She's never had a care in the world, not that one," Alice said as she pulled a day dress from Marian's wardrobe. "The blue or the green today, Lady Marian?"

Marian rose from the bed, pulling the strands of her plait apart as she walked to the dressing-table across the room. Alice already had Marian's most comfortable blue dress in her hand when she spoke. Marian nodded to the bed, giving Alice the signal to lay out the day dress along with her underthings. Alice always asked questions to which she already knew the answers.

Marian began brushing the sleep-pressed waves from her blonde hair. Unlike Cecilia's, Marian's hair was not pale blonde or luminous. It was darker, more like the colour of straw. It didn't glow, it just looked dead and flat. It never seemed to catch the sun or shine in the lamplight at a ball. Everything about Marian felt like a rough imitation of Cecilia: her eyes were blue, but a light, unsettling colour that made her look far too clever to be trusted, her cheeks and jaw were pale and angular instead of rosy and round, and she never attracted others like Cecilia did. It was almost as if everything beautiful got used up in Cecilia and all that was left for Marian were the rough and faded bits.

Cecilia was life and warmth personified and Marian was practicality and stability. No man craved that, or wanted to tie themselves to it. Which was why Cecilia was marrying someone she was deeply in love with, a good man who had loved her back all his life, and Marian would remain alone.

Knowing our differences, and my future, is better than false hope, Marian thought as her hands twisted that hated hair into a tight bun at the back of her head.

Marian saw Alice watching her carefully in the mirror and managed a smile to her maid.

❋❋❋❋❋❋❋❋❋❋

The Fullers arrived precisely as Daniels predicted. The family, and essential household staff, lined up outside the house to greet their guests. It had been several years since Marian had seen Robert Fuller, but he was much as she remembered. His dark hair had gone grey in some places, but his bushy moustache was as black as it had ever been. Marian knew little of their business arrangement. Only that Lord Denbigh provided substantial financial backing to factories Robert Fuller purchased in New York. While the other peers and Englishmen of class were slow to turn to trade and the acquisition of capital to save themselves, enterprising Americans were always eager to join in profitable business ventures. Lord Denbigh also kept a close eye on the progress of Fuller's management of the factories over the years. The two men had traveled back and forth between New York and Warwickshire several times, but Fuller had never brought his daughter along.

When Katherine Fuller stepped from the back of the sleek black Wolseley, Marian was momentarily stunned. She expected someone who looked younger. Who looked less well put together. She planned for a young woman who lacked experience, who just needed some smoothing around her unpolished American edges, not a woman who looked like she'd seen much more of the world than Marian ever had. Katherine Fuller looked positively dangerous. Her dress was too tight, her face was painted with lipstick and rouge, and her hair was so short it bounced around her ears. Her hips swayed gracefully as she walked toward Marian. *A reputation, indeed.*

Some instinct buried deep in Marian's gut told her to run toward that destructive flame rather than away. Good sense told her to hide in the kitchens until Cecilia's wedding was over and the Fullers had gone back to America.

Introductions were made, but the words sounded like they were coming from underwater. Marian's eyes focused on the inappropriately red shade of Katherine Fuller's lips as she smiled. That bright, blood red colour against the shocking white of Katherine's teeth was too much and she couldn't look away.

Lady Denbigh led the party into the house and directed the staff to take the Fullers directly to their rooms. Marian followed dutifully behind their guests, watching the way Miss Fuller's entirely too snug dress clung to curves Marian had never even dreamed of having. After the Fullers were led to their rooms, Marian made a quick escape to her own room and leaned heavily against the closed door. Her heart beat wildly in her chest and her palms were damp with sweat. That black pit of longing she felt when she looked at Cecilia and Henry opened just a bit wider in her stomach. She was not prepared for the kind of trouble Miss Katherine Fuller seemed ready to stir.

Marian needed to reformulate her strategy for dealing with Katherine Fuller, and quickly. She had planned to befriend Miss Fuller, to show her through example the proper way for a young woman to behave. Marian no longer thought a gentle, friendly approach was the best tactic. She needed to be more direct. She needed to employ a stronger hand with the obviously willful Miss Fuller.

There was a seed of admiration in Marian's response to Miss Fuller's arrival, but the threat of her father's disapproval was too strong. Remembering how Miss Fuller looked when she stepped from the car, how her tinted lips pulled in a smile, made butterflies take flight in Marian's stomach. She quashed them. That admiration would need to be held down for the next few weeks, and then Miss Fuller would be gone and Marian wouldn't need to worry about her again.

Luncheon went smoothly. The men discussed business while Lady Denbigh and Cecilia attempted to pull Miss Fuller into conversation about the wedding preparations. Marian watched as Miss Fuller nodded and smiled politely at all the correct places in conversation without actually joining in. Marian knew what pretending to be interested in a conversation looked like, she did it often herself, and it seemed to be a skill Miss Fuller had in spades. Marian caught Miss Fuller sliding glances her way during breaks in conversation, but was quick to look away. It was best not to encourage such behaviour, even if Miss Fuller's looks had all been subtle. But even subtle made Marian's stomach clench in a way that didn't quite feel like fear.

The men retired to Lord Denbigh's study shortly after finishing their plates while the ladies moved to the family sitting room. Cecilia, by force of will, pulled Marian and Miss Fuller to a sofa near the center of the room to finish a conversation she had started with Miss Fuller over luncheon. Marian had overheard bits and pieces of talk about Cecilia's wedding over dessert but hadn't paid enough attention to join in now. But it seemed as if Miss Fuller was in no hurry to continue the conversation either.

Miss Fuller's smile was bright. Those impossibly red lips were barely dulled by the punch served at luncheon. "I've heard quite a bit about your grounds actually. I wonder if Lady Marian would take me for a tour since the weather is so nice?"

Cecilia was far too wrapped up in her own world, as always, to see the request as an outright refusal to participate in any more wedding conversation. Miss Fuller was good at this. Better than Marian expected.

"I'd love to, Miss Fuller. The garden is not at its best this early in the year, but I'm sure you'll enjoy it." Marian had no choice but to honour her guest's request. That it had the advantage of getting her out of any more wedding planning was fortuitous. Marian couldn't be too upset over that.

"Wonderful. I'll grab a shawl and meet you outside." Katherine Fuller left the room as if she never intended to wait for a response.

Marian tried very hard not to compare of the glint in Miss Fuller's eyes to that of a cat with a canary in its sights.

✿✿✿✿✿✿✿✿✿

"I'm sorry, but I couldn't take another moment of wedding talk." Miss Fuller looped her arm through Marian's as they exited the house. She was shorter than Marian, her shoulder brushing against Marian's upper arm.

Marian tried to shift away, to leave more space between them. "It's quite alright, Miss Fuller. I would prefer to walk than spend more time in the house this afternoon."

"Please, call me Kitty. Everyone does."

"That seems very informal for someone I've just met," Marian tried to make her tone like a stout matron handily setting down a young upstart. Instead it was more of a sputter. She'd have to practice that. It wasn't necessarily improper, especially among young women, to use given names or nicknames, but Marian felt a creeping sensation along her spine when she looked at Miss Fuller. A polite distance needed to be maintained.

"Katherine, then. At least until you're convinced that we're friends. And we're going to be friends, right?" Katherine slid back into the space Marian had created between them, letting her shoulder rest along Marian's arm again. "My father said you were given strict instructions to keep me in line while we stay here."

"My father thought it was best you have someone to keep you company you while you stay with us." *Why would Mr. Fuller tell his daughter that? Why would Father have told Mr. Fuller that either?* Marian prided herself on being able to think quickly on her feet, to avoid social faux pas, but Katherine Fuller was proving to be a challenge. It didn't help that Marian felt off balance, like she was tilted slightly to the left all the time, around Katherine. Nothing she said sounded confident enough. None of her actions seemed decisive enough. She led them to the garden entrance, head held deliberately high.

They entered the gardens with Katherine still holding her arm. The gardens definitely were not at their best. The winter blooming plants were drooping and dry but the spring flowers had not yet broken through the soil. The garden looked washed out, dead, and not at all the kind of place one wanted to spend an afternoon. Katherine didn't seem to take notice of the plants at all.

"Can they see us here? From the house?" she asked.

Marian took a quick glance back at the looming building. If all parties were still in the rooms they retired to after lunch, they should go unseen. "No, the sitting room and Father's study are both on the opposite side of the house."

"Thank God." Katherine quickly pulled a cigarette case from the front of her dress. Marian wasn't sure where Katherine could have hidden that in a dress so tight. "Smoke?" Katherine said, holding the open case out to Marian. Inside were two rows of neatly arranged cigarillos.

"No." Marian was deliberately short with Katherine while she struck a match.

"Daddy has such a problem with me smoking cigarillos. He thinks they're too masculine. I don't think he'd care if they were regular cigarettes." Katherine turned her hungry smile back on Marian, this time quirking only one side of her mouth but still giving off the same aggressive feeling. Back to being the cat and the canary. It made Marian shiver. "But where's the fun in that, hm?"

"You'd upset your father purposely just to smoke cigarillos over cigarettes?"

Katherine blew out a long trail of spicy smelling smoke. "Yes, of course. They taste like clove and oranges and anise. I like them, so why should I give them up? Just because he says I should?"

"That's generally how daughters should behave, yes." Marian's annoyance rose at Katherine's obvious disrespect for her father. She took a deep breath, willing her voice to stay neutral and calm.

Katherine only laughed. "Oh, I do like you. You and I will be friends." It was as if Katherine were needling her on purpose.

"You're very sure of that."

"Yes, we're very much alike." Katherine took another drag from her cigarillo.

Marian gave her a very deliberate up and down look, channeling all the coolness she could muster and taking in the short, dark hair neatly curled around Katherine's face, the stain of lipstick and rouge on her skin, the dip in the front of her dress that framed her collarbones, and all the way down the outline of her curves to where her shoes peeked out beneath her hem. "No, I don't think so."

Katherine was quiet until she finished her cigarillo and flicked the exhausted stub to the ground. "Trust me. I'm never wrong about things like this. And we're going to be spending a lot of time together." Katherine turned and headed down the garden path leading farther away from the house. "Now show me the best of this dreary collection of plants."

It was as if Katherine didn't care at all about the distance, the very necessary distance, Marian was trying to build between them. The realisation that Katherine was getting under Marian's skin but not the other way around was aggravating. Marian had to suck a deep breath through her nose before going after Katherine. She would not trail behind in her own family's garden.

Marian's longer stride caught up to Katherine quickly. "The wedding is only a few weeks away. The time will go by faster than you think."

Katherine glanced at Marian but kept walking forward. "Do you know why we're here so early?"

Marian paused. The quick turn in conversation caught her off guard. She did not know how much Miss Fuller knew about their situation, how tenuous it might be. "I was told that our fathers have business to discuss."

"Yes, that's right!" Katherine beamed with pride up at Marian. "After a fashion, anyway." Katherine stopped again, checking back over her shoulder to make sure the house was out of view completely. "Our fathers are planning to expand their operations here in England. They'll buy at least one factory and turn it over to your new brother-in-law to manage. I'm sure my father and I will be staying in England long enough to get it up and running before heading back to New York."

Marian's mouth opened in shock and her eyes went wide. Henry had no experience in business, and expanding when money was tight seemed like a reckless strategy.

"Don't worry. I doubt we'll be staying at Warwick Paddox House that entire time. Once the factory is secured, I'm sure we'll be moving to wherever it is for the rest of our time in England," Katherine threw in before walking away again.

"That's not what I was worried about." Marian called after her, staying rooted next to a mostly-dead rose bush.

Katherine turned but didn't walk back to Marian. "Then what were you worried about?" Her voice rose to be heard across the grass and stone path separating them. It was a bit unladylike, but Marian couldn't say she minded.

"How do you know all of that?"

"Because I refuse to stand idly by. Women like you and I must make our own futures, Marian. Our fathers won't give it to us and we won't marry into it."

Maybe that was too much to shout across the garden.

Marian could feel her brows come together and etch a deep V above her nose. Katherine walked back toward her. She didn't stop until she was close enough to Marian that she needed to tilt her chin up to look Marian in the eye properly.

Marian looked down at her for a moment before licking her lips and saying, "You intend to go into business instead of marrying?"

The question felt too judgmental even as Marian said it, but she had no words for anything else she wanted to ask. She wondered how Katherine could make her own future without a husband, or maybe even her father supporting her. Certainly women did that all the time, but not ladies or the daughters of the nouveau riche. Poor women who lived in reduced circumstances and who had no other choice lived that way. Marian wanted to ask how it was to be done. She was too afraid to ask why Katherine thought she was that kind of woman too.

"I intend to make my own way." Katherine slid her hand along Marian's arm and took a step to the side. Marian was still trying to gather her thoughts from Katherine's outrageous declaration of independence but the trail of gooseflesh Katherine's fingers left along her arm made that difficult. Katherine looped her elbow with Marian's again and pulled them close. They walked in silence past several rows of withered roses and hydrangeas.

Those moments of silence gave Marian time to calm the riotous emotions churning in her stomach. It was unlike her to be so ruffled. It felt as if something was going unsaid, something she almost understood. She pulled them to a stop in front of a manicured flower bed where a few brave daffodils were beginning to peck through the soil. She dropped Katherine's arm as they stopped. "I thought, perhaps, your father was bringing you here to look for a husband." Marian remembered her father's words about Katherine alienating all good company in New York and it seemed logical to assume Katherine would be on a husband hunt while in England.

Katherine's laugh was loud and unrestrained. Marian couldn't help but smile along with her, pulled into some sort of agreement not by the topic but by the freedom in Katherine's laugh. "No, my father is wise enough to leave me to my own personal affairs." It seemed like an odd deflection of Marian's question, but Katherine sobered quickly and pressed on before Marian could ask anything else. "What about you? Do you think you'll marry? After all, your older sister is just now tying the knot. There's plenty of time for you, if you want it."

Marian sighed. "I prefer things the way they are. Cecilia was lucky to find a good man who loves her. I can't begrudge her that."

Katherine made a face. "Of course you're happier the way you are. You have your own life, your own pursuits. Who wouldn't want that? Maybe women like you and I are happier without husbands."

"Maybe." It was the first time Marian had let herself think of her impending spinsterhood that way. It was always an eventuality, never a choice she was making because it was the best one for her. But what would happen to her if Warwick Paddox House needed to be sold? If her parents couldn't afford to keep her on anymore? Being unmarried was suddenly more daunting than before. Katherine was not going to make Marian's task easy.

"See, I told you we were alike." Katherine's smile was bright and sharp again. "Come on. I'm tired of your dreary garden. I think I can put up with polite company again."

"Aren't I polite company?" Marian almost giggled, suddenly feeling light headed, as they turned back on the path leading to the house. Katherine Fuller made her unsteady. She felt impish and wary in rapid turns.

"No, I don't think you are. But that's all right. I prefer it that way." Katherine slipped her hand into the crook of Marian's elbow again. The warmth from Katherine's fingers sunk through the damp spring chill. This time, Marian was the one who brushed their shoulders together.

"I never told you that you could call me Marian." She wanted to sound stern, to pull them back to their purpose and to propriety with one sharp reminder. Her words came out much more like teasing. One walk in the garden and she felt close to failing at her task.

"No, but I fully intend to anyway." Katherine glanced at the vacant space where flowers would soon grow. "Do you grow violets in your garden?"

Marian's step faltered. "I don't know. Maybe in some of the shadier spots. We may have walked past some and not noticed."

"Oh, I would have seen them. I always notice violets." Katherine tilted her head up to watch Marian's face. "You should grow violets. You'd look lovely in them."

Chapter 3

She had no time to see Katherine privately. It felt cowardly to breath a sigh of relief at that, but Katherine had been a shock to Marian. She had seen Katherine at dinner and then in the sitting room each night. Katherine talked quietly and politely with Lady Denbigh and Cecilia, and even sometimes Marian, but she was nothing like she was in the garden.

She didn't laugh like the sound needed to be released from her chest in order for her to keep on breathing, she didn't smile like she was calculating the best way to talk you in circles, and she certainly didn't smell like cloves and oranges and anise. Marian hated it. Every polite moment felt like a lie.

As Marian wrestled with the guilt of avoiding Katherine, Katherine sought her out. Which Marian should have anticipated, really. It was a grey and rainy afternoon and the families were gathered in the sitting room. The men were sequestered in one corner. Lord Denbigh no doubt wishing they could excuse themselves to his study or some other more masculine retreat, but Lady Denbigh would have none of it.

Marian had excused herself to a window seat across the room from where her mama and Cecilia chatted over needle point and Katherine read a book. Instead of joining in, Marian watched the rain with a magazine in her lap. Afternoons like this had lately made her feel listless. The sun was weak and the rain trickled down as if English summer had come early. It was a comforting thing to watch, until Katherine tapped her on the shoulder.

"Did I scare you?"

"Just surprised me." Marian ran a hand over her face and looked up with a forced smile. She and Katherine weren't truly alone, but an intimate conversation was what she had been trying to avoid.

Katherine sat down next to her, perched on the edge of the window seat. Marian pulled her legs back automatically, politeness winning out over the desire to be alone.

"I'm bored." Katherine said.

She sounded like a petulant child and Marian smiled genuinely at that. "Rain is boring. Other than books or parlour games, there's not much else to do in the countryside when it rains."

"Parlour games are terrible." Katherine pulled a very unladylike face, tongue half out and eyes scrunched up. Marian laughed. Not loudly enough to draw attention to them from others in the room, but enough that Katherine heard and answered with a dazzling grin.

They sat quietly for a few moments, the listlessness she had felt fading away, until Katherine nudged her by bumping their hips together. "Take a turn about the room with me?"

She laughed again, this time loudly enough to earn a quizzical look from her mother. "A turn about the room? You sound like an Austen heroine."

"I've read Austen." Katherine stood, waited for Marian to follow, and then looped their arms together.

Marian followed her lead, walking slowly around the outside of the room. "This isn't really what we do on rainy afternoons, you know."

Katherine shrugged but kept them moving forward at a leisurely pace. "I'm experiencing English culture. I thought this is what you did. Secretly shared confidences right in front of nosy matrons and the like."

"You would get that impression from reading Austen. To be honest, I can't imagine you enjoying her books."

Katherine slowed them a bit, stretching out their circuit of the small room. "I didn't. See how well you know me already? I read them, I didn't like them. The ladies are always too passive. They have dreams. They plan and they scheme but in the end they have to just wait for something to happen. No one does anything."

"That's not true at all."

"Fine, they do something but it's not enough."

"But you're going to do something that will be more than enough." Marian could already hear the echoes of their conversation in the garden coming back to her. But instead of talking of such wild new ideas in private, they were now whispering about it with heads bent close together in front of both of their families.

Well, if the Dashwoods or Bennets could share secrets like this, surely Katherine and she could talk for a few moments. Even if they were acting out a ridiculously outdated social dance. Katherine didn't seem to mind. In fact, she seemed delighted. Marian's heart kicked up a notch in her chest at how genuine Katherine's happiness seemed.

"Of course I'm going to do something. Something grand." Katherine smiled up at her. Marian wanted to pull back. They were so very close. "No one is just going to give us anything, Marian. You have to make your own adventure."

Adventure was such a flippant way to refer to one's future. It seemed disrespectful somehow. Or at least foolhardy to treat life altering decisions as mere adventures. It made Marian bristle. "I think you should take your own fate a bit more seriously."

Katherine shrugged, her shoulder rubbing along Marian's upper arm. "I'm very serious about it. I'm just not grave. You can take something seriously without being dismal."

Marian didn't believe her. But, already, she knew there was no arguing with Katherine. She stayed silent as they turned to walk down the final length of the room. Lady Denbigh and Cecilia had glanced up at them a few times with bemused expressions. Marian's cheeks heated with embarrassment the closer they got to where their families were seated.

Suddenly, Katherine pulled her to the side and crowded them behind a tall potted fern. There was no way they would go unnoticed here. Marian rolled her eyes. "What are you doing? Everyone can see us."

Katherine smiled her bright, ferocious, real smile. "So? It's just our families. They don't matter. It's not like we're creating salacious gossip in public."

Marian felt a stab of heat strike her core thinking about that. She pushed it aside. "What are you doing, Katherine?"

"You have to make your own adventure, Marian." Katherine grasped both of her hands tightly and pulled them up high, holding them in the small space between their chests. "You know what Austen's heroines all had in common? They figured out what they wanted before the end of the book. They didn't wait until the end of their story to lament being unhappy. Don't do that, Marian. Please."

Katherine was pleading with her. Pleading behind a fern in her family sitting room. Over a silly idea that had never popped into Marian's mind. Her path was set. She had finished with seasons. She would stay in the country and take care of her parents and the estate. She would help them keep their home if she could. That was her future.

It seemed to pale in the reflection of Katherine's dark eyes gazing up at her. Marian wasn't built for adventure, unlike

Katherine. Marian could easily picture Katherine conquering any task she put before herself. It stirred something in Marian. Something rebellious and something that wanted to push back. Maybe Marian could aim for a bit more adventure as well.

"All right. I'll try." It came out as a whisper. Marian couldn't look away from Katherine's deep, serious eyes.

Katherine squeezed her hands before letting them fall. "Good. Figure it out, Marian. I know you can." She stepped from behind the fern and left Marian there confused and alone.

That conversation stayed with Marian over the next few days. Katherine didn't seek her out again, but Marian watched as she became more quietly rebellious. Katherine wore dresses that were cut a little too low or fitted just a little too tight across her hips. Her lips were always red. There was a budding pride growing in Marian for Katherine's one obvious public display of rebelliousness. However, Lady Denbigh and Cecilia didn't find it as harmless as Marian did.

"She should be ashamed, presenting herself like that." Lady Denbigh said. She, Cecilia, and Marian were in the family room looking over flower orders and taking a late morning tea on the first truly sunny day they'd had since the Fullers arrived.

"I'm sure she doesn't know what she's doing, Mama. New York must be very different than England, and she's had no mother to guide her." Cecilia's defence of Katherine was both backhanded and sincere. She had never been the best at thinking of others charitably.

Lady Denbigh paused in her perusal of the bouquet samples laid out on the table before them, pondering that for a moment. "Perhaps. It would be difficult growing up with only a father. Especially when he's a businessman and rarely is at home. She was often away at school and I think that could make a young girl lonely."

From Marian's seat next to the window, she spotted Katherine walking from the front of the house, heading down the path toward town. Marian thought Katherine was anything but lonely. She seemed to enjoy her solitude and find no burden in it. It looked very different to how Marian felt about her own life.

After a few quiet moments of tea sipping and an occasional comment over the quality of hot house roses, Lady Denbigh came back to the subject of Katherine. "It was a good idea for your father to put her in your care, Marian. She obviously could learn a lot from you."

Marian gave a quick, polite smile. "Yes, Mama." She rose from the window seat, smoothing her dress as she stood. "Please excuse me. I have some correspondence I should tend to before it gets too late." Their casual dismissal of Katherine, their patronising attitude toward her, was too much for Marian to listen to anymore. It scratched against her skin and made her uncomfortable. It made her feel guilty because she had felt that way too, before she met Katherine.

Marian went directly to the front entrance of the house and straight down the path leading to Warwick Paddox. If she hurried, she could catch up to Katherine. The desire to be around Katherine pushed Marian forward. After spending time with her mother and sister, Marian craved her honesty. She cut across the drive leading to the house and followed the path as it bisected the grass. The path led through a copse of trees before passing a pond.

Marian made it to the edge of the pond before she heard Katherine call out to her.

Katherine was sitting on a blanket in the soft grass that edged close to the pond. She sat near the water, several metres off the path. Marian smiled as she picked up her skirt to avoid a stained hem and made her way Katherine's side.

"What are you doing out here?" Marian stopped by the edge of the blanket, looking down at Katherine's upturned face. Just seeing Katherine, Marian knew the polite veil she had worn in front of their families had dropped away and Marian was immensely glad. Seeing Katherine's obvious relaxation made the tension slip off Marian's own shoulders. The sun was warm on her cheeks and she already felt happier.

Katherine turned away to blow a puff of smoke from her cigarillo toward the pond. "Hiding."

"But you called me over. I might have walked right past you."

"So I did." Katherine looked back up at her and shifted slightly, making room on the blanket. "You might as well sit down, now that you're here."

Marian settled herself on the open space next to Katherine, angling herself away so that their arms did not touch. It was a silly thing to be aware of, but it felt important to Marian to maintain a bit of distance. Even though she had sought Katherine out. She silently watched the insects gathering around the pond reeds and listened to the birds while Katherine finished her cigarillo. Marian took a deep breath, allowing the spicy smell to cloud her lungs. She felt the anxieties that had been building in her since her last private chat with Katherine fall away. Knots that had formed between her shoulder blades loosened and Marian tipped her head back to enjoy the sunshine. Everything was quiet except for the sounds of nature around them.

Katherine shifted beside her and Marian turned to find Katherine staring at her. The intent, dark eyed gaze made her uncomfortable. She felt hot along her collar bones and her palms prickled with sweat. Heat gave way to a chill that skated down her spine. Marian cleared her throat and began to stand. "I can go, if you'd rather be alone. If you're really hiding."

Katherine's hand grasped Marian's arm just below the cuff of her shortened sleeve. Katherine's hand was uncomfortably hot on Marian's skin as Katherine tugged her back down to the blanket. "No, I like having you here. I'm not hiding from you."

Marian's cheeks reddened at the compliment. "Who are you hiding from?"

It felt disingenuous to ask, since Marian had been hiding from Katherine for several days. But Marian still wanted to know. She seemed to want to know many things about Katherine Fuller.

"Everyone else. Everyone I have to keep myself hidden from." Katherine sounded despondent and tired. She laid flat on her back, extending her legs off the edge of the blanket. Her shoes and stockings had been discarded before Marian arrived and her toes wiggled in the grass. Marian looked away from the pale curve of her ankle.

"You don't seem very much like yourself in the evenings," Marian ventured, keeping her eyes focused across the water.

Katherine hummed and tucked her arms behind her head. Marian tried to keep her gaze forward, but stole glances from the corner of eye. "Being around others for so long is draining."

"It's not just that, though." Marian looked back at Katherine's reclining form. Katherine's dress had ridden up even farther and the tender flesh of her calf was exposed. Katherine's skin looked cool and inviting. It was harder to look away this time, so she kept her eyes locked with Katherine's. Marian could feel clarity settling over her, as if she was almost understanding something vital about Katherine. Almost, but not quite yet. "You're not the same as you were in the garden. You're not what I expected."

"What did you expect?"

"Someone different." Marian hadn't found Katherine to be at all inappropriate or misbehaved. Well, maybe a bit misbehaved, but certainly not offensive. She was more... untamed, but not uncontrolled. Quite the opposite. Katherine seemed to carefully control what side of herself she presented to others. It just wasn't always the side they expected to see.

Katherine closed her eyes and smiled up at the sky. "Good answer. We think alike. That's part of the reason I told you we're the same."

"Only part of the reason?" The pit in her stomach seemed to be opening more and more these days. Sometimes with butterflies dancing there and sometimes with just the yawning emptiness, cracked apart just a bit at the casualness in Katherine's statement. Marian craved something more than that from Katherine. Something she couldn't put words to.

"Yes." Katherine tilted her head in the general direction of the empty space next to her. "Lie down. Enjoy the sunshine with me for awhile."

Marian kicked off her shoes and lowered her back to the blanket. She willed the pit to close itself, for the butterflies not to come, so that she could enjoy this time. "You don't seem like the kind of person to enjoy lying around doing nothing."

"I'm not. Not if there's better trouble to get into."

"Ah, there's the Katherine Fuller I was expecting to meet." Marian laughed at the indignant huff Katherine let out. "I suppose you'll just have to resign yourself to several weeks of no trouble in the idyllic English countryside."

Katherine rolled on her side. She bent her elbow and rested her head in her palm to look down at Marian. "Do you think so? I think I can find a way to entertain myself before we leave Warwick Paddox."

"I'm supposed to be setting a good example for you, remember?" Marian stayed stretched out on her back but turned her head to meet Katherine's eyes. Katherine's face was so close that Marian almost rolled away.

"The best possible example. I'm just a terribly slow learner. I've always been too stubborn for my own good." Katherine bent her knees until they bumped against Marian's leg. She brought her bare toes forward to rest them on Marian's stocking covered feet. "Don't you think I can find trouble here?"

Marian turned her head to look up at the sky. She took a deep breath, which was much easier to do when she wasn't looking at Katherine. Her mind focused on the pressure of Katherine's knee against her leg and the feeling of Katherine's toes flexing against the top of her foot, though she tried to think of anything else. "No. Warwick Paddox, maybe all of Warwickshire, is devoid of mischief-making."

"That sounds like a challenge." Katherine's toes began a slow climb across Marian's foot, her knee sliding higher along Marian's leg, stopping just above Marian's ankle. Marian's cheeks felt hot and she had to suck in a breath in one long, shallow pull. All of her nerves, her whole world, narrowed down to where Katherine's toes dug into her stockings and Katherine's knees pressed against the outside of her thigh. The hem of her dress had been raised just an inch or so by the movement of that knee.

Marian searched for something, anything, to ground her. She remembered the conversation that pushed her to follow Katherine from the house in the first place and grasped for it like a life preserver. "Is that what you did while you were at school? Found trouble?"

Katherine's toes stop their slow progress but stay firmly pressed to Marian's ankle. "How did you find out that I was away at school?"

"My mama told me. She thinks it made you lonely." Marian kept her face turned to the sky, but it was a struggle not to look at

Katherine. It was not like her to spill out the confidences of conversation with others, especially when it could be something hurtful. But she was compelled to tell Katherine. Marian had wanted to tell her a lot over the past few days, just wanted to speak to her about anything at all. Katherine was quiet for a few moments and Marian could feel Katherine studying her profile. Then, Katherine laughed.

That laughed pulled Marian's gaze from the sky and back to Katherine's face. With Katherine curled on her side, their faces were only a few inches apart. Katherine's deep brown eyes were locked on Marian's and she was still smiling.

"You don't mind that people talk about you?" It seemed strange to Marian, who had been brought up to fear gossip and the damage it could do to someone's reputation.

"Not really. Especially when they get it wrong." Katherine kept her eyes locked with Marian's and her lips quirked up at the corners, twisting her broad, open smile into something mischievous.

"What did she get wrong?" Marian focused on a light dusting of freckles across Katherine's nose rather than spend more time looking into her eyes. It felt too close, too intimate.

"Only the important bits." Katherine's toes flexed and Marian's attention pulled back to those tiny points of pressure against her stocking. Katherine continued, "I loved being at school. I was never lonely. I found myself there."

Marian's eyebrows dipped toward the bridge of her nose in confusion. "You were lost but not lonely?"

"Never lonely, and not really lost. Just…misplaced for a while." Katherine's voice stayed upbeat and happy. Marian would have felt uncomfortable talking about something so personal, but Katherine gave no signs of embarrassment. Katherine's toes flexed against her ankle. "But I didn't find trouble. It found me."

"I'm sure you were just an innocent bystander." Marian kept her voice as light as possible. It felt important to keep the moment inconsequential, though Marian was unsure why. It felt as if they were on the edge of something and too close to falling over it. Katherine's breath slid across her cheek. "You did nothing to instigate trouble, surely."

Katherine's eyes crinkled at the corners while her smile grew even larger. "I may have had something to do with it. Once I figured out what kind of trouble I was interested in. I told you, I found myself at school."

"And what kind of trouble did you find?" Marian's breath caught and she held Katherine's gaze. Her curiosity felt dangerous but it could not be contained.

"Hopefully the same kind I'm going to find here." One of Katherine's feet wrapped around Marian's ankle, holding her leg in place while Katherine's other foot slid just a bit higher on Marian's shin.

Marian's mouth went suddenly dry. Her shin and ankle pushed back against Katherine's feet without her conscious command. "I told you, there's no trouble to be found in Warwick Paddox." She sounded breathless.

Katherine was quiet. It was a queer stillness that Marian was beginning to associate with Katherine. She held Marian's gaze and her feet remained pressed to Marian's leg. Marian stared back, only brave enough to hold Katherine's gaze for a few moments, before quickly turning her face back to the sky. "We should go back. It will soon be time to dress for dinner."

"Alright," Katherine said as she rolled to her back, pulling her feet away from Marian. "Time for polite company again. I think I have the energy to keep my mask in place."

Marian sat up and looked back at Katherine's supine form. "Why do you bother?"

"I'm rebellious, not self-destructive."

"Are you really rebellious, though? I've not seen you do or say anything terribly shocking." A spike of anger flared through Marian's chest, fueled by conflicting, confusing feelings. Katherine was pleasant and kind in public and oddly sweet and fun. Katherine put careful thought into her future, and she may be a bit unconventional, but she was nothing like Marian's parents thought she was. Marian was unsure if the anger was at Katherine for hiding herself from everyone or for letting Marian see a glimpse of who she might actually be. "You act as if you have this reputation behind you, everyone says that you do, but you're nice and kind and fun to be with. I don't understand you."

Katherine sat up quickly, wrapping her hand around Marian's forearm with a firm squeeze. "There you are! That's the spirit I knew was in there."

Marian leaned away but Katherine kept her hand closed around Marian's arm. "What do you mean?"

"We're the same, you and I. We play along because we know we have to, but we're both looking for a way to carve our own path. To be our own people. You do it within the existing host of rules and regulations for your sex and your position. I tend to be a bit more creative. But we have the same purpose, just different paths to get there." Katherine rose to her feet and pulled a very confused Marian up after her. She turned and walked toward the house, leaving Marian to gather up the blanket.

"No, that's not what I want. You misunderstand me," Marian said when she caught up to Katherine. Marian shortened the stride of her longer legs to match Katherine's pace.

"No, I don't. You may not realise it yet, but I'm right." Katherine stopped and Marian pulled up sharply next to her.

"Are you lonely, Marian?"

Marian wished they were back on the blanket so she could look away to watch the sky or just roll away and leave Katherine there alone. Standing next to Katherine with the first grass of spring tickling her ankles, she felt trapped.

"I don't know," Marian said quietly, unable to look away from Katherine. "Cecilia thinks I am."

Katherine stepped closer. The breeze made Katherine's hair flutter across her cheek. Marian wanted to reach up and brush it away.

"I don't think you are. I think you're just misplaced." Katherine smiled brightly, as if they weren't having the kind of conversation that left Marian feeling raw and open. "You can find yourself too."

Katherine took her arm, like she did for their first walk through the garden. "I'll find us some trouble before I leave Warwick Paddox House and then you'll see."

Marian indulged in the very unladylike habit of rolling her eyes. This was a regular conversation with Katherine. She could handle that. "You aren't going to whisk me away for something improper and suddenly convince me that I have been hiding a rebel inside myself all along."

Katherine made an amused humming noise. "That's exactly what I plan to do." They came out of the trees near the pond with the large house looming in front of them. "But not today. Today it's back to the status quo. Is your stiff upper lip firmly in place?"

Marian couldn't help but smile. She was wonderfully content in the spring sunshine with Katherine's teasing voice in her ears and the warmth of their arms hooked together. "Always," she teased back.

"But it shouldn't be." Katherine's voice was quieter, more serious as they drew closer to the house.

Chapter 4

Several rainy evenings later, Katherine read a portion of *Much Ado About Nothing* to both families gathered in the sitting room after dinner. Everyone was obviously entertained by the story, but Marian was enthralled watching Katherine read. Katherine was transformed. She was radiant. She was the most like herself that Marian had seen in the presence of others. Marian stood by the window enjoying the light sound of the rain tapping against the glass and letting the rise and fall of Katherine's voice wash over her.

Marian had spent days trying to watch Katherine without being seen. She still thought about what Katherine had said while they lounged on the banks of the pond. Was Marian's quiet reluctance to marry, to follow the traditional path prescribed for her, the same as Katherine's more obvious defiance? Were they really cut from the same cloth, not lonely but misplaced somehow? Being able to watch Katherine so openly was a gift.

Katherine finished the scene and put the book aside. The gathered families clapped politely and complimented Katherine while she ducked her head demurely. Marian could see the beginnings of that mischievous smile curling the corners of Katherine's mouth. The put-on show of genteel and ladylike behaviour was a joke in itself. Now it was a joke Marian could share in. Katherine caught her gaze from under lowered lashes and Marian felt her own smile grow.

It took a few moments before Katherine could extract herself from the rest of the party to join Marian by the window. They stood quietly, watching the rain for several long minutes. It washed the shared joke away and left just the two of them in a room full of distracted background players.

Marian shifted so her shoulder brushed Katherine's before speaking. "I enjoyed your reading. *Much Ado About Nothing* has always been one of my favourite plays."

Katherine laughed genuinely, but not her regular great guffs of laughter that would have drawn attention to them, and skimmed her fingers across Marian's sleeve. "I've always preferred the tragedies myself. They seem more realistic."

"Surely you don't think all of life is a tragedy?"

"Oh not all of it. But probably the most important parts. It's in tragedy that things really happen. Comedies feel so mundane."

Marian smiled. It wasn't the tragedy itself that Katherine craved, just the dramatic action. "With how frequently you laugh, I would have assumed you loved comedy."

Katherine shrugged, but left her hand resting on Marian's arm. "I would have guessed you liked tragedies. They match the gloomy atmosphere in England."

"I think either can tell a compelling tale. The trick is to find something about the characters that feels familiar."

Katherine's head tilted to the side and her eyes narrowed. "Do you think you're too wise to woo peaceably? Is that why you're on the shelf so soon?"

"That sounds more like you than me." They stood so close together, Marian had to tilt her chin downward to look in Katherine's eyes. Katherine's fingers moved, slowly tracing the inside seam of Marian's sleeve. "You're far more aggressive than I am. I can't imagine how you'd react to a suitor."

Katherine's fingers stopped just below Marian's elbow. She squeezed, her nails catching on the fine lace of Marian's gown. "Why would you assume I wouldn't be the one doing the courting? I couldn't wait passively for someone to come along and do it for me. I told you the Dashwoods and the Bennets waited too long and did nothing. Not me."

Marian wanted to push her arm more tightly into Katherine's grasp and she wanted to move away at the same time. Katherine made it very hard to breathe when she stood so close, when her casual touches became more intent. Marian stayed still but her heart beat faster against her ribs. "I can't imagine there are many men who would be pleased to find themselves playing second fiddle in their own courtships. It bodes ill for marriage."

"Second fiddle?"

Marian sighed. "You know exactly what I mean."

"No, I don't suppose there are many men who would be content with that." Katherine dropped her hand, but its warmth lingered on Marian's sleeve. It felt as if Marian had failed some sort of test she hadn't know she was taking. Katherine's withdrawal left only disappointment behind. "I'm not interested in a husband. I told you that when I first arrived."

Marian thought back to their conversation in the garden on that first day, her mind trying desperately to keep up with the conversation over the pounding of the blood in her veins. "I thought you meant you weren't looking for one on this trip, or here in England, not that you weren't interested in marriage at all." Marian was perplexed. Katherine might be outspoken and less refined than some women, perhaps, but that made her capable of holding excellent conversation. Not to mention that she was beautiful, with dark hair and darker eyes set against a roses and cream complexion and ample curves Marian thought any man would desire. Surely Katherine could chose one man that respected her independent nature out of the many that would no doubt flock to her. There probably were even men looking for that rebellious spirit in a wife. Marian began to say so but Katherine cut her off entirely.

"I know I could find someone suitable. A man that I may even like, but it's not for me. I'd rather look for something better."

"Something better?" The question dropped from Marian's mouth before she was able to pull it back. It left her spinning. All a young lady should want was marriage to a man who liked her, maybe even loved her. There were some who decided on, or resigned themselves to, a different path. That included Marian, but there was nothing better about that. It was just the best some could do.

"Something better," Katherine affirmed. "Something much more troublesome." The wicked smile was back on her face, matched by the mischievous glint in her eyes. It was an expression Marian had only seen when they were truly alone, the expression she had begun to think of as for her alone, now on display in the sitting room with the rest of their families only a few feet away. Marian glanced over Katherine's shoulder, but the rest of the party was engrossed in conversation and not paying the two of them the slightest bit of attention. Katherine caught Marian's look back to the rest of the room and her smirk deepened. "Speaking of trouble, I've found us some."

Marian's eyes darted back to Katherine's. "What?"

"I found us a bit of an adventure. Nothing too scandalous, just some fun."

"Trouble or an adventure?" Marian's mouth was dry and her tongue stuck to the roof of her mouth.

Katherine's eyes twinkled. She was practically bouncing on her toes. "Oh, the best adventures are always a bit of trouble too."

"Did you have to scour all of Warwickshire?" Marian tried to hide her nervousness behind the glib comment. But Katherine saw right through her.

"No, I barely had to dig into Warwick Paddox. It's a side of your sleepy village you never knew existed." Katherine lowered her voice and touched Marian's arm again. "It's nothing dangerous or terribly improper. I won't let anything bad happen to you, Marian. I swear." Katherine's voice was serious and the twinkle in her eye had grown hard. It was a promise.

At Katherine's sincerity, Marian's anxiety lessened and a cautious excitement rose in its place. It didn't feel strange to trust Katherine in this. It didn't feel strange at all. "All right." Marian paused and glanced back to her parents and sister on the other side of the room. "Are we going now?"

Katherine smiled, not her devilish smirk, but a more wistful smile that Marian couldn't help but return. "That's my girl. Ready to rush into danger." She dropped her hand from Marian's arm again and took a step away, leaving enough space for the air to come rushing back to Marian's lungs. "It'll be a few days. We'll go at night. Don't worry, I'll come for you. I wouldn't leave you behind now."

✿✿✿✿✿✿✿✿✿✿

Breakfast was tense. Lord Denbigh and Mr. Fuller were bent over correspondence that had come from the solicitor early that morning. Mama kept glancing at them with her mouth set in a deep frown. Even Cecilia was quiet and contained.

Marian barely picked at the food in front of her. She wanted to ask, wanted to know, what was wrong. Her father would never tell her. Mama would be shocked that Marian would step out of line so far as to ask. She'd be shushed and put in her place without ever knowing what was happening.

For the first time in her life, Marian felt a hot flush of anger paint her cheeks at that. Katherine wouldn't have kept her tongue if she really wanted to know. She would have demanded to be told, would have pushed and cajoled until her father let her know the bad news. Marian couldn't do that. Even now, with a feeling deep in her gut telling her to act, she couldn't do it.

Katherine had taken a tray in her room. She wasn't there to help Marian. She also wasn't there to see how ashamed Marian was that she couldn't demand to know the state of family affairs.

"Mama and I are going to town to buy some ribbons for my veil today," Cecilia said to no one in particular.

Lord Denbigh's head shot up. "If you keep going, this wedding will bankrupt us!" He slammed his palm against the table. "Have some sense, girl!" Lord Denbigh yelled and stalked out. Mr. Fuller stopped only long enough to mutter an embarrassed apology to the ladies before chasing after him.

There was an astonished pause from everyone around the table. Cecilia's eyes were as round as saucers, Mama looked away, and Marian stared at the empty doorway. Daniels ushered the footmen out with whispered orders.

She had heard her father shout before, but never like this. There was anger and an edge of desperation in his voice.

"Maybe I don't need new ribbons."

Mama squeezed Cecilia's hand. "Oh dearest, it's not the ribbons."

Marian opened her mouth to ask what exactly it was then, but closed it as tears started to spill down Cecilia's cheeks. Instead, Marian excused herself and escaped to her room while Mama comforted Cecilia. They hardly noticed her exit at all.

The curtains in her room had been pulled back to let in the weak spring sunshine. The room suddenly felt like a haven from the outburst at breakfast and the overhanging uncertainty that made Marian's stomach clench.

Something unfamiliar caught her eye. Tossed in the middle of her covers was a scrap of folded paper. She opened it, thinking that maybe a maid had dropped it while making her bed.

Inside was a sketch of a rose. Short, sharp pencil lines overlapped to shape its petals and gentle curves formed its leaves. Marian smiled at it and stopped herself from running her finger over the drawing. It wouldn't feel like spring roses blooming but she wanted to try it anyway.

It was likely that one of the maids, maybe even Alice, had dropped it. That one of them had a sweetheart who drew them pretty pictures. Marian found it sweet, even though Daniels would disapprove. She had to take it to him anyway. He would want to know if one of the maids was being courted.

Chapter 5

"Daniels, may I speak with you?" Marian stood in the doorway of the bustling kitchen, hands folded neatly in front of her.

Everyone stopped. The cook, the kitchen maids, the footmen, everyone. They stared at her for a moment before Daniels clapped and broke the silence with one short, sharp crack. They all jumped back to work and looked away, eyes downcast.

Marian turned, cheeks turning red, and tried to keep her head high as she led the way to Daniels's office.

He closed the door softly behind them and waited. Daniels would never bring up Lord Denbigh's outburst, and Marian was in no mood to talk about it. She only wanted to move on.

She thrust the folded, jagged-edged note at Daniels. "I think one of the maids is receiving gifts from a young man."

Daniels's eyebrows rose as he took the paper from Marian and carefully unfolded it. "It's a well done drawing."

"It is. I don't want to get any of the maids in trouble, but I thought you should know." Marian chewed her bottom lip, suddenly concerned the unlucky maid might lose her admirer. "And...I think you should give the drawing back to her, whoever it belongs to."

"Where did you find this, my lady?"

"It was left on my bed. I found it after breakfast." A lump rose in Marian's throat at the reminder of that morning.

Daniels looked up, a bit shocked, and held the paper a fraction of an inch closer to her. Not enough for her to be compelled to take it from him, but closer nonetheless. "Lady Marian, are you sure this wasn't intended as a gift for you?"

Marian's mind went blank. She hadn't considered that. She felt foolish and a flush spread across her face. The only person who would have done that was Katherine. With whom she had shared the sad garden and lain in the grass by the pond.

Hope swelled, stretching from the pit of her stomach through her chest. Katherine would have just handed her a sketch of a flower, not tried to deliver it secretly. But the idea of secret notes being passed and Katherine's secret, sly smile made that hope bubble into Marian's throat.

Her instincts told her to quash that feeling, to run from it and be afraid. She looked at the scrap of paper in Daniels's hand, but did not take it.

"No. No, it's not meant for me." Marian backed toward the door. "Please find who it belongs to and don't give the girl too much trouble."

She definitely did not flee the butler's pantry.

✿✿✿✿✿✿✿✿✿✿

The next note was a sketch of a bird, done in thick, charcoal lines. It was on a piece of paper barely larger than the first scrap Marian had found. It was tucked into a book she left in the library the night before.

Marian discovered it only a few hours later. Katherine had been keeping to herself all day and Marian was suddenly struck with the image of Katherine sneaking around the house hiding bits of paper for her to find.

It was fanciful and ridiculous and Marian could almost see Katherine doing just that. But not for Marian. It was the kind of game schoolgirls would play on a rainy day. Maybe if they had been childhood friends, Katherine could be reminding her of a game they used to play. As it was, there was no reason for Katherine to sketch small, delicate things and leave them for Marian to find.

Marian yearned for there to be a reason.

She stood in the library, book long forgotten, and dragged a finger tip along the rough edges where the bird had been torn from the rest of the paper that once held it. It was no bigger than Marian's palm and it felt fragile in her hands.

"Do you like it?"

Marian jumped and nearly collided with Katherine. She had snuck up behind Marian as quiet as a mouse.

Marian's heart beat heavy in her chest, partly from the fright and partly from fear. "Is this yours?" She held the bird out to Katherine in her open palm.

"No, it's yours." Katherine's white teeth stood out sharply next to her painted red lips.

"Why?" If Katherine hadn't been standing so close to Marian, too close, she may not have heard. Marian was quiet and breathless.

Katherine shrugged and stepped back, just an inch or two, but it was enough space that Marian could think more clearly. "I like to draw and I like you."

She said it so simply. As if it were just a statement of fact and not a mystery. It answered none of Marian's questions and only caused the butterflies living in her stomach to stretch their wings in anticipation.

"Do you often draw for your friends? For your family?" This time Marian took a small step back, but Katherine took a larger step forward. The hand in which the bird rested was still stretched between them. Katherine was so close that Marian had to curl her fingers to keep from brushing Katherine's chest.

Katherine smiled, sweet and wistful. "No, I haven't wanted to draw for someone in a long time." She shifted just slightly and the satin of her dress brushed the back of Marian's bent fingers. "But I'll draw more for you."

Marian wanted to retreat. Katherine's touch was warm against her hand. "No, you don't have to do that. The bird, and the rose too, are lovely." She wanted to run back to Daniels and demand the rose back. "I'm sure they took you some time to make."

"I'm stuck in the country. What else do I have to do?" When Katherine breathed, her chest came forward and Marian's fingers brushed the underside of her breast. Neither of them moved. "I'd draw you if I could but I've never been good with people's faces. Can never get the nose right."

Marian should draw her hand back, but she couldn't. She left it there, not moving backwards or forwards. Letting the rise and fall of Katherine's lungs be her excuse.

They stared at each other in silence for seconds, Katherine just breathing and Marian trying to keep her hand from moving. She wanted to twist her wrist, wrap her hand around Katherine's ribs, and crush the bird between them. If she did that, her thumb would be where her fingers were now. She could move it, slide it along...

Katherine stepped back and Marian's hand fell to her side, sketch fluttering to the floor.

"You should keep those. I could be a famous artist one day."

Katherine's voice was strained and soft in a way Marian had never heard before. Maybe she wasn't the only one struck breathless.

Chapter 6

It was pitch black outside when her bedroom door opened. Marian woke immediately, her heart beating fast. Katherine said it would be a few days. Had she come for Marian already?

Marian sat up in bed, ready to push her coverlet to the floor. "Katherine?"

Cecilia's voice whispered through the dark. "Marian? Are you awake?"

"Cecilia? What are you doing in here?" Marian breathed a small sigh of relief as the immediate fear of being pulled into Katherine's plan so soon faded. But part of her wished Katherine was here to take her off into the night. She wouldn't have minded being woken up for that.

"I can't sleep." Cecilia made her way to the side of bed.

Marian pulled down the edge of her coverlet to beckon Cecilia in. "We're not girls anymore, Cecilia. You can't come to sleep with me whenever you have a bad dream."

"Why not? It's always worked before." Cecilia crawled in and let her cold feet curl under the hem of Marian's nightdress. "Why did you think I was Miss Fuller?"

Marian's voice caught in her throat. It wouldn't be improper, well not terribly improper, for Katherine to seek Marian out at night if she had good reason. Maybe if she was ill or had had a bad dream. But 'an adventure' wasn't a defensible reason. Marian had no good way to respond without admitting that she just hoped

Katherine Fuller would come to her bedroom in the middle of the night. Instead, she teased, "You'll be married in less than a week. Married ladies can't sneak from their beds in the middle of the night."

"Maybe by then I'll have a better reason to stay abed." Cecilia sounded so knowing, so experienced when she said it that Marian blushed. Thankfully the darkness provided adequate cover as Cecilia continued, "And I didn't have a bad dream. I just couldn't sleep. Nerves, I suppose." Cecilia settled in next to Marian, turning to face her.

Marian smoothed a hand across Cecilia's hair. "The wedding?"

Cecilia nodded her head. "Yes, and no. I'm positive I want to marry Henry. I can't wait to be his wife. It's just getting there that's making me uneasy." Marian remained quiet and gave Cecilia a few moments to collect herself before she continued. "I just want everything to go perfectly. To be perfect."

"It will be. Everyone is so happy for you, and Henry will be so pleased when you marry." Marian let her joy for her sister pour out through the comforting words.

Cecilia's smile caught what little light shone through the windows. "I know, and I'm grateful. For you, for Mama and Father, and for Henry. It's just..." Her voice went quiet and the silence hung between them while Marian stroked her hair. "I know everyone will be happy and the day will be lovely but I want it to be perfect for me. Is that terribly selfish?"

Marian kept her hand smoothing Cecilia's hair back, as if she were an upset child. "No. It's not selfish. It's your special day after all."

"I knew you'd understand. You'd never hold such selfish thought against me."

Cecilia's eyes were beginning to drift closed when Marian said, "Stay here tonight. It'll be my last chance to keep your bad dreams away."

"I was supposed to be the one to do that for you, you know. You were supposed to be the younger sister who came to me when you were uneasy."

Marian laughed quietly, lips pressed against the crown of Cecilia's head. "Well, we've got it a bit backwards but it's worked for us, hasn't it?"

Cecilia's voice was slow, already sliding into sleep. "You've just never been uneasy. Even as a girl, you didn't need me like that."

Marian was quiet but stayed awake until the sky turned a pink tinged grey. It had always been enough to comfort Cecilia, to be there for her sister, but her mind kept turning to Katherine. Suddenly, it didn't feel like enough anymore.

✿✿✿✿✿✿✿✿✿✿

The next someone who snuck into Marian's room under the cover of darkness wasn't Cecilia. The wedding was only two days away and the calm night did not reflect the moods of the Warwick Paddox House inhabitants.

Despite the seed of longing for Katherine's company that had taken root deep in Marian's gut, she never dreamed she'd wake to Katherine's fingertips pressed to her lips.

"Shush, it's just me." Katherine's voice was quiet and her fingers slid across Marian's cheek as she pulled her hand away. "I've finally worked up that surprise for us."

Marian struggled to relieve herself from the heavy comfort of sleep and her blankets all at once. "I think you waking me in the middle of the night is surprise enough." She rubbed her knuckles across her eyes before sitting up.

Katherine had abandoned Marian's bedside in favour of pulling clothes from the wardrobe. Marian's dresses were being scrutinised and discarded with shocking speed. "Don't you have anything that you can move in?"

Marian scurried from the bed. "What are you doing?" She snatched a pink and cream day dress from Katherine's outstretched hand.

Katherine looked Marian up and down before meeting her eyes. Marian must have imagined Katherine's gaze lingering on the shadows showing through her thin nightdress. "You need to get dressed. That one will have to do." Katherine's smile cut through the dark bedroom and Marian was struck by a moment of lightheaded giddiness. This was exactly what she had been missing.

"I can't wear this one. It doesn't fit." She gestured across her chest and felt her cheeks turn pink. "It's too tight for polite company."

Katherine's smile grew wider, devilish in the dark. "We're not going out in polite company." She waved off the complaint gathering on Marian's lips. "Skip the corset. You won't need it."

"Then it really won't fit," Marian grumbled.

Katherine laughed, light and bubbly, and squeezed Marian's arm. "Get dressed. I'll be right back." She slipped from the room, leaving a bemused Marian behind. She hadn't even thought to ask where they were going, but refusing Katherine was unthinkable.

✿✿✿✿✿✿✿✿✿✿

When Katherine returned, Marian had almost accomplished the task of getting dressed on her own. Her wardrobe really wasn't designed for it. Even her simplest dresses had hooks or buttons she couldn't reach. Katherine eased the door shut as quietly as possible before turning to Marian. "Are you ready?"

Marian quickly pulled her hair into a messy bun at the back of her head. "Ready for...." Her voice dropped away as she took her first proper look at Katherine. "Are you wearing trousers?"

Katherine looked down at her own legs. "I need to be able to move. You're going to slow us down enough in that." She gestured back to Marian's very practical day dress.

"I will not." Without knowing where they were heading or what they'd be doing, Marian was already defensive about her ability to keep up. She wanted to be able to keep stride with Katherine, both physically and in the whirlwind of quick-witted conversation that Marian has come to expect from Katherine. She was driven to match Katherine, to be her equal. "I'll be fine and where did you get trousers?"

Marian had seen trousers cut for ladies before. But Katherine wore trousers cut for men, stretched tight across her thighs and tucked messily into ladies' boots. A rough lawn shirt in dingy white was tucked sloppily into her trousers. It hung off her shoulders, obviously too large, which made the trousers look tighter by comparison.

"I borrowed them from one of your stable boys. Bit snug though." Katherine rubbed her hand low across her abdomen, where the fabric stretched to accommodate her hips. Marian watched Katherine's hand move back and forth across the taut trousers and tried to distract herself by checking the tightness of her bun against her scalp. She looked back up at Katherine's face to find her smiling. "At least we'll both have too tight clothes."

"The fit isn't why yours are impolite." Marian was being snide. She couldn't help it. Her eyes were drawn back to where Katherine's fingers still played low across her stomach.

Her snideness was met with exasperation. "It's not that sort of bash. You'll be the belle of the ball, straining stitches or not, and I won't be the only lady there in trousers." Certainly, she meant lady in only the broad sense of the word.

Marian turned away, partially to take her eyes away from the drag of Katherine's fingers and partially to quash the growing urge she felt to reach out and touch Katherine herself. She gestured to the half-fastened row of buttons on her back. "Could you?"

She felt Katherine step behind her, close enough that Katherine's breath warmed the skin across the back of her exposed neck. They stood there, quiet and still, for several moments until Katherine finally reached up to fasten the remaining buttons over Marian's shoulders and neck. She lightly ran her fingertips, the same ones that had been pressed to Marian's lips when all this began, over the edge of Marian's chemise. Her trailing hand left a ribbon of warmth over the sensitive skin between Marian's shoulder blades.

Katherine snapped her hand back and Marian immediately felt cold, bereft of Katherine's touch. She quickly pulled the fabric of Marian's dress together and slid the buttons home. "There. All done up and ready for a night on the town."

Marian didn't turn around as Katherine stepped away. Instead, she ran damp palms over the front of her skirt. "Night? It's practically morning." She took a deep breath before turning to face Katherine.

Katherine smiled broadly, rubbing her palms in front of her chest. "We've got hours before dawn. I'll have you tucked back into your cozy bed well before the house is up for the day. Promise."

Marian forced down the answering smile that jumped to her lips. "Where are we going? I can't just go running off in the dark."

"Yes you can. You're a grown woman. You can do what you like." Marian raised an eyebrow and Katherine sighed. "Okay. You can't do whatever you'd like, but you can at least try."

"Just tell me where we're going, please."

Katherine reached out and twined her fingers with Marian's. "Can't. That would ruin the surprise. Just trust me. Please."

The warmth that ran across her back at Katherine's touch now wrapped around her fingers and snaked up her arm. She squeezed her fingers tightly, trying to keep Katherine close. Trust, in the abstract, seemed like such a risky proposition, but when Katherine was holding her hand it felt very right.

Instead of dropping her hand as Marian feared she might, Katherine tugged Marian's hand to lead them quietly through the bedroom door. "We have to hurry. We have a ride to catch."

❁❁❁❁❁❁❁❁❁❁

"Where is he? We're not too late." Katherine mumbled to herself as she stepped onto the deserted road. She stood, hands on hips, squinting up one side of the road and down the other. Marian maintained her post in the shadows. She was careful to stay out of view of the house even though, at this distance, she was sure no one could see her. The cover of darkness raised her hopes. Her trust in Katherine was complete but she still feared the things Katherine could not control.

"Hullo? Miss Fuller?" A voice hissed from several metres down the road causing Marian to jump.

"It's all right. He's our ride." Katherine's hands slid along Marian's sleeves, soothing her from shoulder to wrist and then back again.

"Sorry. I just didn't expect someone to be there." Marian took a deep breath, still determined to stand equal with Katherine's adventurous nature, and squared her shoulders. "I'm fine. Just a little surprised."

The hands fell away from her shoulders and Marian instinctively stepped forward, further into Katherine's space, as if she could will Katherine's hands back to her simply by closing the distance between them. But Katherine turned away and enthusiastically waved her arms above her head.

"We're here!" she called in a hurried whisper. A lantern winked into view, cutting into the blackness in the middle of the road.

"Come on then, Miss!"

Katherine took Marian's hand again and pulled her into the road. Marian gripped Katherine's fingers tightly and dug in her heels. "Katherine. Please. Where are we going?"

At the abrupt stop, Katherine turned and took both of Marian's hands in hers. "Some of the village folk are playing music in a barn tonight. Dancing, drinking, just a good old fashioned blow. It will be fun. And you'll be safe. I promise. Okay?"

Marian's mouth went dry. She knew from the moment Katherine pulled her from bed that something like this was likely. This was not going to be the type of dancing, drinking, or socialising she was accustomed to. Would anyone tell her father?

But she'd come this far and she'd be damned if she was going to slink back to her bed while Katherine went off into the night. "Let's go." Her voice didn't come out quite as strong as she would have like, but it was clear and calm.

Katherine didn't step away. She held Marian's gaze. "I'll look after you." Marian could tell Katherine was trying to be soothing. It was obviously meant to make her feel better, but it was also sincere.

"I trust you," she said. "I mean it."

Katherine's smile was brilliant, even in shadow. She pulled Marian close enough to wrap an arm around her shoulders. She had to stretch slightly to reach around Marian's taller frame. Standing on tiptoe, Katherine leaned close to Marian's ear. "Maybe someday you'll trust me to surprise you."

Her voice was light and teasing and Marian couldn't help but respond in kind. "You're always a surprise."

She tugged Marian toward the waiting cart with a devilish smile. Katherine jumped easily into the back of the cart and patted the straw-cushioned space next to her. Marian pulled herself up more cautiously. Her legs swung off the edge as they jolted forward. There were two young men sitting on the driver's bench urging the lurching horse onward.

"Hullo Lady Marian. Miss Fuller." The voice was familiar and Marian twisted to get a better view of the man sitting on the bench. "It's Edward. I work in your stables, my lady."

Marian smoothed her skirt automatically and smiled her best, most serene smile. "Yes, I recognize you. How is your mother?"

"She's well, miss." The stable boy turned to focus on the road ahead. Marian could hear Katherine giggle, likely laughing at her stilted attempt at conversation with her own stable boy.

When the boy faced away, Marian turned to watch the road falling away behind them. She let out a deep, shaky breath.

"Relax." Katherine bumped shoulders with her. As if they were just walking in the gardens again. "He won't tell anyone. Isn't that what servants do? Keep your secrets?"

Marian rolled her eyes. "You make us sound ridiculous."

"You're the one who slipped immediately into the landed-gentry role."

Marian dropped her voice, careful not to let the men driving the cart hear her. "I just need to make sure my father doesn't find out about this." Just thinking about Lord Denbigh's reaction to his youngest child sneaking out in the middle of the night to attend a country barn party with the very woman she was supposed to be teaching polite behaviour was enough to make Marian's stomach drop.

"He won't. I promise." Katherine looked at her, head tilted slightly upward to accommodate the difference in height that remained even when sitting, and Marian's heart skipped up and down in her chest.

She swallowed and looked away. "You can't make that promise."

"Trust me, remember? The other option was to steal a car, but my driving is rotten." Katherine's shoulder came to rest against hers again. Not a bump this time, but lingering contact. The night air kissed across the back of Marian's neck as the cart moved forward, leaving goose flesh in its wake. But where Katherine's shoulder pressed into her arm, her skin burned.

Chapter 7

The barn was a few miles away, nestled just off the main road on the near side of the village. Marian had walked and rode past it all her life and never looked twice. Now there were lights and loud music slinking through the cracks in the walls.

Katherine jumped to the ground while the cart was still moving. As it lurched to a halt, she reached up to help Marian down. Marian didn't need her help, but she took Katherine's hands anyway.

As Marian's feet landed on the ground, Katherine's hands slid to her waist. She gave a little squeeze. "Are you ready?"

Marian closed her hands around Katherine's wrists with an answering pressure. "Yes."

The music that filtered through the cracks in the barn door drew Katherine's attention. She dropped her hands and that mischievous smile was back. "Good. But first, some light refreshment." Katherine giggled at the parody of the words and Marian found herself smiling in return, in equal parts at the joke and just to see so much joy on Katherine's face.

Katherine unfastened the first two buttons of her fitted blouse and reached into the front of her chemise. The smile froze on Marian's lips. She watched, dumbstruck, as Katherine pulled a small silver flask from against her chest. She had seen a cigarette case fitted snugly there but a whole flask, even a small one, seemed impossible. Katherine even had pockets to take advantage of tonight! And she still chose to fit the flask against her chest. Without re-buttoning her shirt, Katherine tipped the flask back and took a long swig. Marian watched the flesh of her bare neck move as she swallowed.

Marian was still staring at the exposed flesh in the 'V' of Katherine's shirt when Katherine offered her the flask. She definitely didn't want to think about Katherine's breasts.

"No, thank you." Marian automatically fell back on the learned politeness of her station.

"Believe me, the night will be much more fun if you have a drink." Katherine pushed the flask into her hand and Marian tipped it back without a pause to second guess herself. Katherine inspired recklessness in her. Katherine smiled as Marian winced against the burn of hard spirits in her throat. Hard spirits that tasted like an old Christmas tree. It was vile. "That's my girl." Marian felt her cheeks heat at the praise.

The horse cart crawled away, going to rest behind the back of the barn, and Katherine turned away to wave at the boys driving it. Marian watched her, the way her hips twisted in the borrowed trousers, the exuberant motion of her upraised arm, and how the light from the oil lamps hanging outside the barn doors perfectly outlined her curves as she twisted back to face Marian.

Katherine grabbed Marian's hand, eyes twinkling in the dim light, and Marian felt warmth pooling low in her gut. Happiness made her dizzy. Happiness that she was here, with Katherine, and that Katherine wanted her here.

Marian tipped the flask back again, the burn expected this time but no more pleasant. The taste seemed more tolerable. Katherine took the flask back and arched an eyebrow.

"Why, Lady Marian. I didn't take you for one who overindulges." Katherine did her best impression of a scandalized society matron before tipping the flask back for a much longer swig.

She passed the back of her hand against her mouth to wipe away any escaped liquid. That shocking red tint Marian had come to love stayed firmly in place, with maybe a little smudge by the corner of her mouth. Marian watched the drag of Katherine's lips with more interest than she cared to admit, even to herself. Tucking the flask into her trouser pocket, but leaving the buttons of her shirt undone, Katherine again laced her fingers tightly with Marian's and pulled her toward the barn.

The music was loud. Much louder than Marian was expecting. It was a brash, tin-like sound, and there was no melody she could pick out. A makeshift band with dented and dirty instruments stood in the corner while couples danced on the cleared out main floor of the barn. Men and women slid and slithered against each other to the beat and clang coming from the band. The confusion, and maybe even horror, must have shown on her face. Katherine was laughing at her.

Leaning close, nearly touching the shell of Marian's ear, Katherine said, "It's jazz!"

Marian turned her head, bumping her cheek against Katherine's nose. "It's what?"

"Jazz! Not as good as New York, and nowhere near what you can hear in Chicago but it's still jazz!"

Marian had no idea what Katherine was talking about, but she seemed so excited. Marian couldn't ruin that with her ignorance. She just smiled and nodded her head instead.

Katherine pulled back, putting distance between them. She motioned Marian toward the makeshift dance floor. "Come on!"

Marian kept her feet firmly planted and shook her head. Katherine continued to beckon her toward the mass of party goers, but she remained resolute. Did this many people even live in the village? They must have come from miles around.

After a few moments of teasing glances and encouraging smiles, Katherine gave up. She took another swig of the flask before tossing it to Marian. "You'll need it if you're not dancing!" And, with that, Katherine was gone into the crowd of dancing couples without looking back. She didn't even have a partner.

Marian found a few chairs tucked in a corner, far away from the band but with a decent view of most of the dance floor. She saw Katherine from time to time, popping up draped across the arms of young men or twirling playfully with other young women while their suitors looked on. Marian took another drink from the flask. There was nothing else for her to do.

She had been happy, excited even, that she was sneaking out to spend the evening with Katherine. That she was finally going to see a bit of the troublesome world Katherine seemed to bring with her wherever she went. Instead, she was left sitting on the sidelines with no one for company except an increasingly lighter flask. She didn't regret coming, not exactly, but being left alone made her self-conscious.

Another gulp or two of the now significantly better tasting liquor raised her courage, but before she could bring herself to stop being such a wallflower, Katherine appeared at her side. There was a soft gleam of sweat across her forehead and above her lip and her shirt stuck sloppily to her sides. She plopped down in an empty chair next to Marian, legs spread and stretched out in front of her.

"You really should dance." Katherine let out a long exhale. She was happy and relaxed and for a moment Marian was agonized that she had ever thought of leaving her.

Katherine took the flask from Marian's limp fingers to shake it. The corner of her mouth turned up in a sly grin when she heard the little remaining liquid slosh against the newly opened space inside the bottle. She took a drink and tucked the flask back into her trouser pocket.

"You should see the balls in New York! Entire theatres filled with boys dressed like girls and girls dressed like whatever they want. Some people are barely dressed at all." Katherine smiled and nudged Marian with her shoulder. "Not the sort of balls you're used to."

Marian's cheeks heated, both in annoyance at being left alone and because she could already imagine the scene Katherine painted. Curiosity burned in her. "I don't think anything like that goes on here."

"I'm sure you've got more than one gentleman or tradesman that likes to wear his missus's stockings around here." Katherine nudged her again. This time Katherine stayed pressed to Marian's side, leaning heavily on her shoulder. "I bet I could find us one in London. You really should see it. They pop up all through Harlem and Greenwich back home. People of all stripes come to be relaxed and happy."

"You seem pretty relaxed now."

Katherine shook her head, hair sliding over the exposed skin at Marian's collar. "It's not the same."

They sat in silence for several minutes while the music slowed down around them. At least, Marian thought the music was slowing down. Her head had gone rather fuzzy and it was a bit hard to tell. It seemed less clang-y anyway. The couples on the dance floor slowed down too and many of them were leaning more heavily against each other. Marian giggled to herself, thinking that maybe they had all had too much to drink as well.

Marian glanced down to where Katherine's head rested on her shoulder. Katherine's outstretched legs bounced back and forth to the slower tempo coming from the band and she watched the crowd wistfully.

"I don't know how to dance," Marian blurted out. Katherine turned to look up at her, obviously confused. "Not dance like that, anyway. There aren't any steps."

"Is that why you didn't want to dance?" Marian said nothing in response. It wasn't really the reason, it was a reason but not the one that most sprung to mind, but Marian was not sure she could put why she was reluctant to step out in such an intimate way with Katherine Fuller into words. At her silence, Katherine pressed on. "I can teach you. If you want."

Marian's throat was dry and all she really wanted was the flask back, even if the most sensible part of her knew that was a terrible idea. Before she could stop herself from jumping headlong into other terrible ideas, she was nodding and mumbling "Yes".

Katherine pulled her up from her seat. She was back to her confident, push-ahead self. Marian's feet felt heavy and her head was spinning. Katherine maneuvered her to the edge of the gathered couples and wrapped an arm around her waist, pulling her close. Marian's hands went to Katherine's shoulders, as much for balance as for dancing.

"I've got you. Here, arms around my shoulders, Marian." Katherine's mouth was so close to Marian's cheek that Marian broke out in gooseflesh again. Her arms slid around Katherine's shoulders, bringing them closer together. Katherine began to bob and sway to the music, pulling Marian with her right and left. She hummed along and Marian closed her eyes to better feel the moment between them. They stayed like that for several minutes, Marian eventually resting her chin against Katherine's messy, sweaty curls.

The music picked up speed again and Marian opened her eyes. It felt like waking from a dream. She felt dried out and like her skin was made of paper. The brassy noises coming from the battered band were making her head ache. Katherine turned in her arms, pressing her back flush to Marian's front. She guided Marian's arms from her shoulders to her hips and latched her hands to Marian's wrists, keeping Marian's arms in place. "Your turn to lead." Her voice was not as light or as teasing as Marian had expected. As Marian had hoped it would be. It sounded deep and husky. Their dance was taking on a much more serious tone.

"I don't...I don't know how." Marian looked around at the other couples. No one was looking at them. Some couples were even dancing the same way Katherine had positioned them. Katherine's hands tightened on her wrists.

"Like this." Katherine used the extra pressure on Marian's hands to push her own hips back and forth. "Move me the way you like. The way that fits the music."

It was suddenly way too hot in the barn. Heat came from the bodies around them, from the lamps burning around the dance floor, but most troubling was the heat coming from Katherine's body against her.

She felt the curve of Katherine's hips, felt her breasts pressed between Katherine's shoulder blades, and felt the drag of those damned trousers against her skirt. Marian dropped her hands. "I want to go home."

Marian spun away from Katherine and maneuvered through the edges of the dancing crowd on her way to the door. She moved quickly, focusing only on escaping from the heat and the noise and the closeness of the barn. Katherine caught her arm as she reached the door.

"Marian! Wait! Slow down." She pulled Marian's arm, short fingernails pressing into the tender flesh inside Marian's elbow. "Let me walk home with you."

Marian shook her head and pushed forward, focused only on the fresh air beyond the barn door. Katherine kept up after her, never letting go of Marian's arm. Marian's head was spinning. The cool night air against her face did little good. "No. Stay. I'll ask Edward to drive me home." She heard Katherine snicker and turned to face her, panic retreating now that there was more space between them and the night air cooled her cheeks.

"Edward's more than a little busy at the moment." Katherine bobbed her head back toward the open barn door. Edward was clearly visible, sitting on a bench opposite the band. His arms, and mouth, were quite occupied by the very pretty vicar's daughter.

Marian blushed to what was sure to be an unflattering shade of red and she was thankful the dark kept Katherine from noticing. The vicar's daughter seemed to be doing better than Marian had done in all her seasons in London combined. She certainly looked happier than Marian felt, then or now. Marian realised she was still watching them when she heard Katherine clear her throat.

"Come on. It's not far if we cut through the fields. I'll walk you home." Katherine dropped her hand away from Marian's arm. Marian felt relieved and bereft. Mostly, she felt as if she could finally breathe properly for the first time since Katherine took her onto the dance floor.

Katherine took them away from the road and led the way across moonlit fields. Marian wondered briefly how Katherine had learned her way around the countryside so well, especially in the near pitch darkness, but Marian had been so tied up with helping her mother and sister prepare for the wedding and overseeing the household that she had no idea what Katherine had been doing with her time. That thought stung. They had so little time together already and she was wasting it. The melancholy thoughts and alcohol still rolling through her gut were a distracting combination. Marian's foot caught in a rabbit hole and she stumbled.

She pitched forward but got her feet back under herself quickly. Katherine was back at her side before she completely regained her balance. Marian expected Katherine to reach out, to steady her, maybe to lean toward her, but Katherine kept a respectable distance.

"Are you all right? Did you hurt your foot?" Katherine's voice was subdued. It was not the concerned or emotional outburst Marian expected. Katherine had been so patient, so caring in the barn. The distance between them felt wide but her voice weaved around Marian like a warm blanket. Like a friend offering comfort.

"I'm fine." Marian straightened and felt the world tilt around her. Her head was still spinning and tears welled up in her eyes. "I feel sick." She took a deep breath and forced herself to stay upright. "I'm sorry that I spoiled your evening."

"Oh, Marian." Katherine wrapped an arm around Marian's middle and the world came back into order. She leaned against Katherine, her hip bumping against the dip of Katherine's waist. Marian's head was muddled and her eyelids felt very heavy, but her melancholy seemed instantly lifted. Her friend wasn't angry with her. Katherine still cared enough about her to pull her close and support her for the rest of the walk home. Marian hummed softly and closed her eyes. Katherine shifted so she supported more of Marian's weight. Marian let her, maybe leaning more heavily on Katherine than she strictly needed to. "I should have paid closer attention to how much you were drinking."

Marian tried to shake her head, but the motion only invited more nausea. "No. It's my fault. You were dancing." She rested her head against Katherine's shoulder, slumped to the side so their heights were more equal.

The journey home was slow. Katherine helped her walk the rest of the way, sneaking back through a servants' entrance and up the stairs to her room. Katherine walked Marian to the side of the bed and turned away to find Marian's nightdress. As soon as Katherine let go, Marian slumped onto the bed and began to wiggle under the covers. The mattress felt cool and inviting against the hot skin of her palms and cheek.

"No!" Katherine tried to quiet her laughter. "You need to get back in your nightclothes."

Marian mumbled a response but kept tunnelling into the mass of blankets left behind in her hasty departure a few hours earlier. She'd almost got her legs tucked in when she felt Katherine pull on her ankle.

"At least take your shoes off. Your maid will really ask questions if you have your shoes on in bed." Marian stopped burrowing into her mattress to think about that. What would Alice say when she found her in the morning? In just an hour or two, really? Marian knew that she should care, that she should do everything in her power to cover her overnight activities, but she was just too damn tired.

In Marian's moment of hesitation, Katherine pulled her legs to the side of the bed and began removing her shoes. Marian kicked her legs, trying to pull back from Katherine. "Don't. I'm suppose to be watching you, taking care of you, not the other way around."

Katherine clamped a hand around Marian's knee, holding Marian's leg firm across her lap. "You're drunk." Her voice was fond but her grip unyielding. Marian laid back, head on a pillow and legs stretched out across Katherine's lap, to think about being drunk and what that might mean. She expected to be more philosophical while in her cups, or more enthusiastic. She just felt tired.

Instead of thinking, she ended up closing her eyes and getting lost in the feeling of Katherine sliding off her ruined slippers. The slippers fell to the floor, but Katherine's hands stayed, one wrapped around an ankle and the other pressing on Marian's knee through the fabric of her skirt. The fingers twisted around her ankle and rubbed across the delicate bones there. The touch was so light that Marian thought she might already be dreaming. But, when Katherine's hands fell away, Marian was sure a dream would never leave her feeling so alone.

Katherine tucked Marian's legs back under the blankets and pulled them up to cover most of Marian's dress. Marian opened her eyes to see Katherine leaning over her, peering at her with a soft expression.

"Did you mean what you said?" Marian's voice had grown thick with sleep.

Katherine's brows pulled together and her lips puckered as she tried to remember. "What did I say?"

"When you first gave me the flask. You said 'That's my girl.' Did you mean it?" Marian struggled to keep her eyes open, to watch Katherine's expression.

"Did I mean what?" Katherine's hand brushed fallen strands of Marian's golden hair away from her cheek. The hand stayed there, cupped around Marian's face. Katherine's thumb rested against her jaw.

"Am I your girl?" This time Marian couldn't keep her eyes open to watch Katherine's response. They drifted shut as she sunk further into the soft comfort of her bed.

Marian felt Katherine lean over and brush her lips across her forehead. "You could be."

Chapter 8

Morning came like an explosion. Marian was sure she'd never been more soundly asleep until Alice yanked open the curtains, letting the morning sun stream in. Every noise and speck of light was amplified in her pounding skull. Alice didn't seem to notice that Marian wasn't awake and lounging in bed as usual. Marian pulled the covers high against her chin to keep her dress covered as long as possible.

Alice prattled on about Lady Denbigh and Cecilia and things that needed to be done before the wedding. Finally, the maid stopped pulling garments from the wardrobe and turned to stare at Marian.

"Do you want to dress for breakfast, Lady Marian?"

Marian's throat was painfully dry, causing her voice to sound like sandpaper rubbed against itself. "Yes." She pushed back the covers, bracing herself for Alice's reaction to her clothes. She managed to get both feet on the floor, despite the pressure in her head, before making eye contact with Alice.

"Lady Marian..." Alice's voice trailed off as she took in the mud-stained hem of the too-tight dress and ruined stockings peeking out from beneath it.

Marian cleared her throat, desperate for a glass of water. "I couldn't sleep so I went for a walk. It turned out to be a bit rougher outside than I expected and when I returned I was so tired, I went straight to bed without changing." The lie was just believable enough that Alice didn't question it outright, but she did raise an eyebrow at her mistress. To break the awkward moment of silence, Marian spun quickly around. "Can you please help me dress? I don't want to be late for breakfast." Her head and her stomach both spun too.

Alice quietly undid the row of buttons down Marian's back and stepped away, allowing Marian to slip the dress from her shoulders.

"You should wash up, Miss. I'll bring some fresh water from the kitchen." Before slipping through the door, Alice turned back. "Next time you need a late night walk, miss, I suggest picking a dress you can put on and take off yourself."

All the muscles in Marian's back went instantly rigid. Her gut lurched. Alice knew. She had to know.

Quietly, facing away from Alice and with her dirty dress clutched around her shoulders, Marian replied, "I hope that we can keep this between ourselves, Alice. I am a grown woman."

"Of course, Miss." Alice's tone was not as approving as Marian would have liked.

※※※※※※※※※※

Katherine looked well-rested and calm, already sipping tea at her seat when Marian arrived for breakfast. For a short moment, Marian hated her. The resentment bubbled up and rode a wave of pounding pain through her skull. Her stomach took a sharp turn when she looked at the sideboard laid with breakfast.

She was still staring when Katherine nudged her shoulder. "Drink as much tea and water as you can. See if you can beg off and get a nap this afternoon."

Marian turned and could see her mother and sister tittering away at the table. "Unlikely, considering it's the day before my sister's wedding. How do you look so chipper?"

"Years of practice, my darling." Katherine had never called her that before. It had to be meant in jest but it was affecting. Marian's face warmed and she had to turn back to spoon some egg onto her plate to cover the flush.

"Well, I don't think I will be practicing again anytime soon." Marian tried to keep her voice curt and on the edge of a reprimand. It was the only way she knew to calm the butterflies dancing in her stomach at Katherine's casual endearment.

Katherine chuckled, a deep and throaty sound. "Admit it. You had fun." Katherine kept her voice low but Marian still looked around cautiously to make sure none of the other guests were approaching the buffet.

Marian had enjoyed parts of the evening, even though she shouldn't have. She shouldn't even have gone with Katherine, much less drank or allowed the other woman to tuck her into bed. "I will not admit to anything about last night."

"That's the spirit." Katherine responded as if Marian was secret-keeping for the both of them. Marian had only been concerned about herself. She felt more than a bit of shame about that. Katherine thought they were together in this and she hadn't considered that. "Here," Katherine said, lifting some sausage to Marian's plate. "It's the last thing you want to eat, but believe me, it will help."

✿ ✿ ✿ ✿ ✿ ✿ ✿ ✿ ✿ ✿

The wedding itself came off well. Henry and Cecilia were obviously in love and had eyes only for each other. Their happiness radiated around them. For the first time in her life, jealousy ran hot and sharp through Marian's veins at her sister's happiness. She would never wish anything but the best for Cecilia, and even for Henry, but today her future as a lonely spinster felt like too much.

Marian saw her life clearly spread out in front of her. She would spend the rest of it at Warwick Paddox. She would run the household in her mama's stead, and love her family, but she would be alone.

Most of the wedding and the celebration that followed went by in a blur for Marian. Katherine was sitting somewhere behind her during the ceremony, and was somewhere in the gardens during the refreshments served to their guests, but they never crossed paths.

Late that night, Marian was finally able to think through her emotions more clearly. She was resigned; she was happy to be a spinster. Not even Henry and Cecilia's happiness before the wedding had caused discomfort with that plan. She would have been happy as a spinster. She should have been happy. But something had changed. Now she wanted more.

Suddenly, she wanted to be as happy as Cecilia and to feel as alive as Katherine Fuller.

Marian sat atop her blankets, feet curled under the hem of her nightdress, trying to face what was different now. She stared into the shadows of her bedroom and her brain ran in circles. She wanted to talk to Katherine, to be with her. Marian gathered her courage to make her way to Katherine's guest room, but she did not move from the bed.

Instead, she heard a light knock on the door.

Katherine pushed the door open just far enough to lean her head in. "I'm learning to be more polite. See? I knocked."

Marian met Katherine's weak smile with a similarly uninspired one, even as joy bloomed in her chest. "I thought everyone had gone to bed."

Katherine slid through the crack in the door, shutting it quietly behind her. "I think they have. A few of the men may still be drinking in the library." She crossed the room and perched delicately on the edge of Marian's bed. It was unlike Katherine to avoid taking up space. Marian wanted to grab her and force her to spread out across the bed.

"Your learned politeness doesn't extend to waiting to be invited in, I see." Marian smiled more enthusiastically but the joy did not reach her tone. She sounded tired, listless.

"Do you want me to go?" Katherine frowned, her brows drawing together to create small creases above her nose. Marian wanted to reach up and smooth her thumb across those lines. She wanted to push them away so that nothing ever marred Katherine's beautiful features. She kept her hands locked firmly around her drawn up knees, paralyzed by the conflicting emotions roiling in her head and heart.

"No, I don't want you to go."

Katherine settled more firmly on the bed, taking up a bit more of the space Marian already thought of as hers. "We're leaving first thing tomorrow for Kent. My father is to take on stewardship of a factory newly purchased by your father. When the new Mr. and Mrs. Clifford return from their honeymoon abroad, the factory will be Henry's." She looked away, picking at a non-existent string on the blanket.

Marian's heart pitched in her chest and her throat closed in on itself. "You're leaving?" She knew this would happen. She even knew that Katherine would leave with Mr. Fuller to expand her father's business, but there had been no mention of a factory having been purchased. It had been weeks since Marian had heard anything at all about business matters. She felt the shock like a physical blow. "Kent?" she questioned weakly.

"Yes, the soon-to-be hub of industry, or so they tell me, and then back to New York." Katherine finally met Marian's eyes. "I think it's the last ditch effort to save the business, and maybe this place."

Marian's throat tightened. "Yes, I think it might be too."

"I can't tell you what to do if things go south, but you'll be fine. I know you will. I know you can take care of yourself." Katherine took a deep breath while Marian held her own. "I wanted to say goodbye."

"I don't want to say goodbye." The words rushed out before Marian could stop herself. She snapped her mouth shut and turned away from Katherine.

The house was quiet around them for the span of several heartbeats. Katherine's voice was equally quiet and nearly lost in the darkness when she responded. "I don't want to say goodbye either." She cleared her throat, picking up some of the vibrato that Marian had come to expect from her. "But I do want to tell you something else. Remember the day by the pond? You were trying to get me to tell you what happened while I was at school."

Marian smiled, remembering the trail of Katherine's toes against her shin that afternoon. "I remember. You said trouble found you and it wasn't about being rebellious."

"It wasn't. Not really. I've always been more adventurous than the girls around me. But it wasn't about adventure or excitement. It was about being happy."

"What happened?"

"You may hate me after I tell you. But I want to be honest. It's important to me. It's important to me that you know how I feel." Katherine paused and sucked in a great breath before pushing on. "There was a girl at school, called Margaret. She was beautiful. She had red and orange hair that looked like flames in sunlight and deep brown eyes and freckles plastered...well, everywhere."

Marian's mind spun with questions. Her world narrowed down to just this bed and this conversation with Katherine. In her heart, she knew what Katherine was about to say. She wasn't completely naive. She knew about men who loved other men. If men could do that, why couldn't women? She wanted to shake Katherine, to make her stop talking. Marian needed this to stay only an abstract concept, not a reality. Not a possibility. Especially not a possibility for the two of them.

But Katherine soldiered on, unaware of Marian's growing panic. "She was so sweet, and kind, and... Well, I fell in love with her. Crazy, reckless love and I wore my heart on my sleeve. We were discovered and sent home to our families. It wasn't drinking or sneaking out or anything like that." She stopped, looking anxiously at Marian. "It was love."

"How were you discovered?" Marian was breathless.

Katherine laughed a bitter, sharp laugh. "With my hand up her skirt by the headmistress."

"Oh." Marian's brain stopped whirring away at that image. It was something she could picture far too easily. Jealousy coiled like smouldering rope in her chest. "Is she waiting for you in New York?" Marian managed to keep most traces of jealousy and remorse from her words, but they still sounded sour. It felt like she was losing something before she even had it. Before she had even properly wanted it.

"God, no." Katherine was still laughing. It was a sound of desperate relief. "Our families adopted the tried-and-true method of starving us out of our 'phase.' We weren't allowed to see, or even to write to, each other. I haven't had any contact with her since the day my father drove me away from the headmistress's office."

"Why are you telling me this?" Marian's mind jumped between two possibilities: that Katherine was going to confess love to her or that Katherine was about to say that, despite her unnatural predilection, she could never love Marian at all. Both options seemed terrible. One would break her heart and the other would terrify her.

"Well, it was this or recite the poems of Sappho to you, but that's never been my style. For me at least, it wasn't a phase. My attraction has always been, and will always be, to women. I won't take a husband and pretend to be something I'm not. But I also don't want to spend my time in this world alone."

Marian dropped her knees so that her legs stretched flat across the bed behind Katherine's back. She laid her hands in her lap, fingers knitted together so tightly that her knuckles turned white. She swallowed heavily, forcing the lump in her throat down before her tongue darted out to wet her lips. "Are you in love with me?"

The seconds stretched out like shards of glass between them, fragile but with the potential to cut deeply. Katherine slid her hand along the bed, trailing her pinky finger along the edge of Marian's nightdress. Her hand came to rest next to Marian's knee. She leaned forward and stretched her fingers so her hand rested partly on Marian's thigh, just above the knee, and partly on the bed.

"No, not yet. But I could love you. If you let me." Her hand pressed more firmly against Marian's leg. "I'm not going to give my whole heart away if I know my feelings can't be returned. I told you I wasn't reckless."

Marian's eyes were locked on Katherine's hand. She wanted to will it all the way up her leg, to burn away the image her mind supplied of Katherine and her young lover. She wanted to throw it off, to push Katherine Fuller out of her life completely. The perfect solution would have been to go back in time. To go back to before she met the woman sitting in front of her, before she felt any desire at all.

"I..." Marian snapped her mouth closed. "You're being very serious." It was a deflection.

"Because this is serious."

Marian looked up at Katherine's eyes. Katherine was staring boldly back at her. "I know it is. I like you this way."

Katherine smiled, slow and sensually. "I'll never be too serious."

"Never too serious, no." Marian smiled back. She couldn't help herself. She swayed forward a bit, toward Katherine.

"I don't want you to answer now. You don't have to say anything." Katherine pulled her hand away and Marian jerked forward to snatch it back. She stopped herself before she reached out, but she stayed leaning that much closer to Katherine. "Your father will come to inspect the factory in a few months, before the newly wed Cliffords arrive to take ownership. If you want to see me again... if you want to be with me, come with him. I'll wait for you in Kent. If you don't come, I'll go back to New York and try not to drink myself to death."

"Don't joke about something like that."

Katherine leaned even closer and caught one of Marian's hands again in hers. Marian felt instantly warmer, instantly lighter, as if this touch was meant to be hers. She turned her hand to thread her fingers through Katherine's.

"I don't know what to say." Her desire, the unspoken truth, hidden even from herself was laid bare on the bed between them. She wasn't ready to admit it to herself, even in the most private of her thoughts, but Katherine just stormed in and stripped away all her defenses. It was so very like Katherine to do exactly that.

The squeeze of Katherine's hand pulled Marian from her contemplation. "I don't want you to say anything. Not yet. Just... just think about it, alright?"

"I will. Quite a lot, I imagine. I've never considered this before." At least not in such great detail, but Marian would be lying if she said the idea was far from her mind when her thoughts strayed to Katherine, even before this declaration of attraction and affection. But this was as close to a confession as she could come tonight.

"I know it must be a shock..." Katherine's platitude was cut off by the rough laugh torn from Marian's chest.

"Not as shocking as you might think. I knew something was different... that I saw you differently than other women—"

Katherine let out a deep groan and pulled Marian forward by their joined hands. Her awkward confession of mutual attraction was cut short by Katherine's lips, soft and dry, pressed against hers. Marian's eyes closed automatically and a sigh of relief escaped from between her barely-parted lips. This was perfection. It felt so much better than the kisses two brave suitors had stolen years ago. Those were not unpleasant, exactly, but this felt right.

Katherine pulled back and Marian grasped their hands more tightly together, afraid that Katherine was going to break contact entirely. Afraid that she'd leave, that she'd changed her mind. Her eyes looked darker with their pupils blown in the low lamp light.

"Should I be apologising?" Katherine's voice was soft and warm, a bit insecure. It wrapped around Marian's shoulders like velvet. She felt it send a shiver across her neck and down the back of her nightdress.

"No. Please. Do it again." Marian leaned forward, nearly in Katherine's lap now, eyes locked on Katherine's lips, before she realised what she'd said.

Katherine met her halfway. The pressure was greater this time, but that same feeling of rightness descended over Marian. Katherine's lips were more insistent. Her mouth slanted sideways over Marian's and she trailed her tongue along the seam of Marian's lips. Instinctively, Marian opened for her. The smooth, wet heat of Katherine's tongue grazing along her own pulled a whimper from Marian. She pushed back, tangling her tongue with Katherine's.

The give and take of the kiss, the intimacy of it, made Marian breathless.

Too soon, Katherine pulled back. She rested her forehead against Marian's. "I should go."

"You could stay. For at least a little while." The thought of them being pulled apart and separated by the breadth of England stabbed at Marian's heart.

"That is a terribly dangerous idea." Katherine rose from the bed and made quickly for the door.

"Katherine." She stopped when Marian called out, one hand resting against the latch. Marian followed her to the door and stood more closely than she would have this time yesterday. Katherine practically shook with power of her restraint. Marian appreciated that Katherine didn't reach out to her. She would have gone too willingly. "Is it always like that when you...?"

"No. It's never like that."

"Oh." Marian was both pleased and afraid to hear her instinct confirmed. Kisses were not always that electric. Hope that this was something special, special for both of them and not just special to Marian because of inexperience, took root in Marian's heart.

Katherine reached up to cup the back of Marian's neck. She had to rise on tip-toe to chastely press her lips against Marian's. It lasted for only a few seconds before Katherine pulled away again. "Come to me in Kent, Marian. Please. Come back to me."

Her hand fell away and with a soft click of the latch, Katherine was gone.

* * * * * * * * * *

Marian was unable to go to sleep. She stayed awake throughout the night, alternating between trying to remember the exact taste of Katherine's lips and cursing Katherine for ever coming into her life. What was Marian to do? Her future, previously unquestioned, was now obscured by shadow. By a passion she hadn't considered, and maybe with love she had never conceived of.

Marian dressed in what she could without Alice's help and twisted her hair into a knot on the top of her head. She sat in the chair at her dressing table, staring at her own shadowed reflection in the mirror, until the light creeping into the room made her own face unbearably clear.

As dawn bled into the sky, Marian heard the car pull up to the front of the house. She stood near the window, remaining far enough back that she was mostly concealed by the drapes. It took several long minutes, but the Fullers eventually exited the house. Katherine's back was straight and her shoulders square. She looked stiff and unlike herself. She radiated as much misery as Marian felt.

Katherine entered the car without looking back. Not even a glance in Marian's direction before she was gone for good.

Marian watched as the Wolseley disappeared down the drive, and she watched a little after that as well. She took deep breaths, the first few almost dissolving into sobs. She pushed down and locked away thoughts of Katherine Fuller.

Chapter 9

Raindrops beat a slow and steady tattoo against the window glass. It had rained every day since Katherine left. Never all day, and never more than a sad drizzle, but it rained in snatches here and there throughout the day. It left just enough room for hope that the sun would break through and force the grey clouds away.

Marian had never felt so in tune with the weather.

She wandered listlessly through her old, familiar life. In the weeks since Katherine had walked away without so much as a look back, Marian's thoughts were consumed with her. She thought about the abruptness of Katherine's confession, her departure, and the future they could have together. And the warmth of her lips pressed to Marian's.

She begged off dinner nearly every night with a manufactured headache. She avoided unnecessary conversation with her mama or any of the servants. She had stopped responding to her correspondence and hadn't been to the village since Katherine left.

It felt as if her life balanced on a knife's edge. Her father said nothing about traveling to Kent and Marian longed for him to make his intentions clear. Indecision still wormed inside her chest but at least her misery would have an end. The library had become her solace. She hid there day in and day out, watching the rain and thinking.

Marian was so inside her own head, mulling over every frightening possibility, that she didn't hear Daniels come into the library. She was curled in the picture window, like she used to do when she was a child. Like then, she had a book in her lap but her gaze fixed on the emptiness on the other side of the window.

Daniels cleared his throat and Marian turned to him, eyes blinking owlishly. "Lady Marian, please forgive me for saying so, but you have not been yourself as of late." The butler moved closer to Marian's perch on the window.

"I'm just tired, Daniels."

Daniels stepped closer again, so that he was next to the window seat. He was close enough to reach out and touch her. He did not. He lowered his voice. "I don't think that's true, Lady Marian."

Marian stared at him, mouth coming open to launch a defence that never quite got there.

"I think you grieve for Miss Fuller." The words were out there. Marian's feelings had finally taken shape and been said aloud, and it had taken Daniels to do it for her. She deflated and the wall she had been trying to construct around the hollow emptiness that grew a little bit each time she thought about Katherine collapsed.

Panic rose from Marian's gut and lodged in her throat. He had said it so nonchalantly, as though it were common for a young woman to be so waylaid by the departure of a friend. It was possible that he hadn't guessed the depth of her feeling for Katherine. She wasn't sure of those feelings herself.

Marian swallowed in an attempt to make her mouth feel less like dry cotton and force down the lump in her throat. It bobbed back up almost immediately. She had to tread lightly, not to give too much away if Daniels hadn't already filled in the gaps for himself. "Miss Fuller and I became friends while she was here and there are times when I..."

Daniels's raised eyebrow and downturned mouth clearly showed his disbelief. She was caught. She swallowed again and pushed images of being thrown from the house and disowned from her mind. "Am I that obvious?" she whispered.

"Only to me." Daniels cleared his throat and pulled a small, cream coloured envelope from inside his jacket. "Miss Fuller asked me to deliver this to you."

Marian stared at it for a few beats of her pounding heart. It beat so loudly she could hear it in her own ears. She tentatively reached out to take the letter. The grain of the paper was smooth beneath her fingers.

"Have you kept this from me?" There was no heat in her words. She stared at the letter in awe, unable to look away to meet Daniels's eyes.

"Yes, milady. I apologise. I should have given it to you weeks ago, but I felt you needed...time."

She ran her fingertips across her name, written in swirling ink on the outside of the envelope. "Daniels, what do I do?" She was pleading. She knew it. She couldn't hold back the misery that blossomed in her chest. It bled out through her voice, and her eyes, and the shake in her hands.

Daniels perched on the edge of the window seat, near Marian's feet.. "I cannot tell you." He sighed deeply and clasped his hands in his lap.

Marian finally looked up and Daniels held her gaze. She desperately tried to figure out what he might know and what he simply assumed. It wouldn't be strange for a friend to leave a letter for her, would it? Especially after all the time they'd spent together during Katherine's stay.

Did this letter mean that Katherine wanted to call it all off? Was she disappointed in, or, worse yet, disgusted by what they shared in Marian's room the night before she left? Even Katherine wouldn't be so foolish as to leave a declaration of love with a servant in her father's house. She must mean to break off whatever tenuous agreement they made that night. That hollow void that had plagued Marian since Katherine walked out of the house that morning began to crumble, falling in upon itself in a great avalanche of pain. It was all Marian could do to keep from clutching at her chest.

But what if she didn't? What if this was tangible proof of Katherine's affection? That weak flame of hope stayed the avalanche. Grief stopped falling but it was an unstable barricade. The only way to find out for sure was to open the letter.

Heedless of Daniels, Marian slid a fingernail under the envelope flap and carefully pulled the flap away from the rest of the envelope. The letter fell into her palm with a shake and she read it quickly, then again more slowly, the knot of anxiety in her gut loosening with every word.

> *Dearest Marian,*
>
> *Since I left your room an hour ago, I cannot stop thinking about you. I cannot stop thinking about how relieved I am that you did not push me away, and even more overjoyed that you welcomed me with open arms.*
>
> *I want this to be the only letter between us. I cannot trust myself to write to you in a way that would not arouse suspicion or to receive your letters without running away to Warwick Paddox to be with you.*
>
> *I also want to suspend communication between us so that you will take proper time to think about my proposal. It will be difficult for us to make a life together and I want you to truly know that before you make the decision to come to me.*

We will have to hide in plain sight and conceal who we are. You have probably discovered that hiding is not in my nature, but I will do that for you. I will do almost anything to make this choice easier on you.

So, do not write. Just think. Think about what a life with me would mean.

Always,

Katherine

P.S. I can feel your disapproval at my delivery method from the other edge of this tiny island. Trust Daniels. He is a friend to us.

A hot stab of shame struck Marian. It had never occurred to her to write to Katherine. She was too trapped in her own indecision for that. Communicating via tepid letters seemed far too inadequate to express her feelings for Katherine, and Katherine was too large a presence to be reduced to correspondence.

She re-read the letter once more and something fell into place with Katherine's postscript. She took a longer, more appraising look at her loyal family butler. At the man who never spoke down to her or treated her like a child, even when she was one, and who had become her friend in adulthood. Marian let out a shaky breath, anxiety dissipating in light of a shared secret. "She told me to come to Kent if I wanted... more." Wanted her.

Daniels waited silently. Marian pushed on to fill the void between them. "I miss her, but I don't know what to do." Saying it for the first time, out loud and to another person, was overwhelming. Hot tears spilled from Marian's eyes. For as heartsick as she had been, and as frustrated and confused, this was the first time Marian actually cried.

"Lady Marian, you're miserable. You've been like a ghost since she left." Daniels handed her his handkerchief to dab at the tear trails marking her cheeks. "Go to Kent."

"Father hasn't said anything about going and I was supposed to travel with him and-" Marian stopped and gulped down a deep breath. Now that the truth was out, it flowed fast and furiously from her lips. "It's going to be so hard, Daniels."

"It will be hard either way. Go to Kent."

He said it so straightforwardly, so directly, that after weeks of mulling over the problem, of being lost in her own head, Marian laughed. "It can't be that simple."

He smiled down at her. "Never simple, but you can't go on like this. If you were meant to move on from her, you would feel it by now. Instead, you are continuing to mope around the estate."

"But father hasn't said-"

"Then ask. Tell him you want to go to Kent. I cannot imagine he'll turn over a business investment without seeing it for himself. Don't let him decide your future, Lady Marian."

"Has he made any plans to go?"

"No, not as yet. But that doesn't mean he won't."

Daniels rose from his seat on the bench and knelt next to her, bringing their eyes level. Marian was struck by how reminiscent the pose was of her childhood yet how much older the man had grown. His knees creaked. "You will have to fight for the life you want. Sometimes the fight will be obvious and sometimes more subtle, but you will need to control your own decisions. Don't ever let someone do that for you. Not even Miss Fuller."

"Thank you, Daniels." She had never meant an expression of gratitude more. Some of the weight that had been bearing down on her shoulders lifted. Not all of it, but enough to make breathing easier.

"You're welcome, milady." Daniels hoisted himself from the floor and patted her hair just as he used to do when she was a child. "This also belongs to you." He held out a small, slightly crumpled scrap of paper.

Marian's heart leapt. She knew what was on the other side of that folded note before her fingers reached out to take it. The paper bent back to reveal the delicately sketched rose Marian had found on her bed what felt like ages ago. She traced a fingertip around the thinly inked lines of rose petals.

"Did you know even then, Daniels?" She did not look at him as she asked, keeping her eyes focused on the rose.

"I suspected, milady."

Marian was quiet as Daniels left the library. She remained in the window seat, staring through the glass. Plans became concrete in her mind. She felt a sense of direction and purpose greater than she had felt since Katherine Fuller blew into her life.

✿✿✿✿✿✿✿✿✿

That night, Marian was the first to arrive for dinner. She wore her best, most matronly looking dress. Her hair was done up in a tight and severe knot. She wanted to look as mature and sure of herself as possible. The churning of her gut and the doubt in her heart would be kept a secret.

She had practiced her arguments, written them out that afternoon and repeated them in the mirror before burning her scraps of paper. She waited until the footmen had ladled hot soup into bowls in front of them and returned to their positions by the wall near here Daniels stood.

Marian glanced at Daniels to bolster her courage and put her plan into action. "Father, I was hoping you were planning on going to Kent when Henry and Cecilia return."

Lord Denbigh looked over the rim of his wine glass, seemingly astonished that Marian had spoken. "I am. I like to make sure everything is in order before I turn the reins over, even just to Henry."

"May I go with you? I've never been to Kent and I'd like to opportunity to visit with Miss Fuller more before she returns to New York." Marian was an atrocious liar, even with practice. So instead of lying, she gave him a fraction of the truth. It made her palms sweat.

Lord Denbigh stared at her as if she'd asked for the moon.

Lady Denbigh cleared her throat and Marian's nerves were so shot she nearly jumped. "I think that would be very nice. It would do Marian some good to get out of the countryside for a bit and to see Cecilia again. Girls miss their sisters, you know." Lady Denbigh's support was unexpected, but Marian was grateful for it.

"Very well. We leave in four days."

The tension evaporated from Marian's back and shoulders. Her hands unclenched in her lap. She was going to Kent. He would take her with him. She caught Daniels smiling at her over her father's shoulder and she ducked her head to cover her own foolish grin.

It had been that easy all along. Marian only had to make the decision to speak up and take control. She felt a sudden harmony with Katherine's life philosophy. She was master of her own future and no one else could decide that for her.

And she was going to see Katherine again.

✿✿✿✿✿✿✿✿✿✿

They arrived at the hotel in Kent just before tea. It was the best hotel the area had to offer but far below the quality her father was used to in London. Marian could see him sniff in disdain. She tried not to search the overcrowded lobby for Katherine, but her eyes scanned over the crowd again and again as Lord Denbigh retrieved keys from the front desk. There was no sign of Katherine's dark bob or sly grin or dress too risqué to be fashionable in Kent.

It was for the best, Marian assured herself. Now she could freshen up in her suite before taking tea and seeing Katherine again. Her room was next to her father's but the walls seemed thick and sturdy, and there was no door connecting their suites. She laid out her best dress and a pair of silk stockings to air before dinner. Marian had left Alice at home, in hopes of needing privacy once she was reunited with Katherine. Katherine wouldn't care how she was dressed, she knew that, but Marian still wanted to look as good as possible. To be confident in her own skin and ready to move into her new life with her head held high. To be as confident as Katherine always seemed to be.

Katherine was not at the private tea Marian and her father took in one of the smaller hotel dining rooms. Nor did she come pounding down Marian's door in the long hours between tea and dinner. Marian had stayed in her room, trying to distract herself with a book, in hopes that Katherine would chase her down. Instead, she had to be content with vivid daydreams of Katherine running into her room, of Katherine catching her partially undressed, and of what Katherine would do to make them both late to the dining room.

Marian's imagination could only stretch so far. She could only remember the kisses they'd already shared and stretch her mind to what she knew men and women did together. How that might be applied between herself and Katherine was still a mystery. Thank God Katherine would know what to do. Marian's skin prickled in subtle gooseflesh when she imagined Katherine's hands on her. Thank God for sturdy walls.

When her father escorted her to dinner, this time in one of the larger, more lavishly appointed ballrooms, he didn't notice how her hands shook with anticipation.

Katherine was there, and Marian spotted her at once. Marian pulled in a great, shaking breath at how lovely she looked. Her hair was sleek and shiny, held down with a blue and silver band. Her dress was the same sky blue and left her arms covered only by loose ribbons of fabric. It glimmered in the low glow of the electric lights as her body moved.

Marian stared at Katherine, watched Katherine smile politely at a young man who pulled out a chair for her, as Lord Denbigh steered Marian to sit opposite Katherine. Marian stayed perfectly still as the noise in the dining room faded around them. She held her breath, afraid to call attention to herself or end this perfect moment of observation. She was poised on the edge of the rest of her life. Her heart was raw and open but surprisingly peaceful in this temporary purgatory of the unknown. One look from Katherine would push them one way or another and nothing would be the same afterward. This moment felt much like the few blissful seconds one experiences in free fall as one goes over a waterfall. Treacherous and exhilarating.

Then Katherine looked up, properly settled into her chair with the young man still trying to dance attendance on her, and her polite smile froze. Marian did not dare say anything as they stared across the long, narrow table at each other. If they both reached out, they would be able to entwine their fingertips next to their empty wine glasses. But Marian did not trust herself to speak without giving away her secrets to the room at large.

Katherine's frozen smile melted into a wide, toothy grin as she looked at Marian. Her eyes were warm and a subtle flush spread across her cheeks. The tip of her tongue darted out to moisten her bottom lip before she mouthed a silent "hello." It was acceptance. It was acknowledgment and joy and want as clearly as could be conveyed at a public supper. The sounds of casual conversation filled the room as the blood rushed back to Marian's head. She ducked her face in relief. Katherine loved her and was hers. Words didn't feel necessary. Marian understood Katherine's heart.

Marian spent the rest of the meal trying to keep up with the discussion of her table partners. It was simple and uncomplicated prattle and she wanted nothing more to beg a headache and go to her room, in hopes that Katherine would find her there. Instead, as the pudding was served, Marian felt a slight pressure against her foot. Thinking it an accident, the natural hazard of long legs and a narrow table, she pulled her crossed ankles back but that gentle pressure followed and became more insistent. Marian's eyes shot up to meet Katherine's light and teasing gaze across the table. How Katherine was managing to press her foot against Marian's without sliding out of her chair, Marian could not fathom. She didn't even appear to be slouched in her seat. But the quirk of Katherine's lips and slight drag of that foot against Marian's left no doubt in her mind as to who the culprit was.

Marian swallowed a large sip of her wine and moved her ankles forward again, to make it easier for Katherine to reach her. It was unseemly and dangerous. They were getting away with something right under the nose of polite company but more importantly, it was fun. More fun than Marian was sure she had ever had at a dinner before and she had barely done anything at all. Katherine filled her with lighthearted joy. She felt giddy with it.

The game came to an abrupt end when the hotel owner, who was hosting their dinner, announced that the men were welcome to adjourn to a private salon for cigars and brandy while the ladies were encouraged to take sherry or tea in another receiving room. The chairs scuffled around them as the other patrons rose. The press of Katherine's foot disappeared and a young man offered Katherine his arm as she rose from her seat. Marian absolutely could not sit politely in a salon and sip at a drink without immediately running to Katherine.

"Father, I have a bit of headache and am overtired from our travel. I'll retire for the evening." It was an excuse Marian had used frequently lately, but it was the quickest one she could think of.

Lord Denbigh, who had spent much of the meal in discussion with Mr. Fuller, creased his brow in concern. "Are you sure you're simply overtired? You seem sickly lately."

Marian gave her father her best serene smile. "Yes, it's nothing. I'll be fine in the morning."

His concern was genuine, if fleeting. Lord Denbigh had already turned back to Mr. Fuller. Mr. Fuller was more sympathetic and sent Marian a concerned look.

Katherine was caught up in the exodus of people from the other side of the table. Marian managed to catch her eye and hold it for a moment. But it was enough. At least it felt like enough to Marian. She could only trust that Katherine would correctly interpret the message. Katherine gave her a slow nod, her face carefully neutral but eyes full of an expectant heat, before exiting the room with the rest of the ladies for their after dinner drink.

Once everyone had abandoned the dining room, Marian let out a long, slow breath and sagged against an empty chair. Her hands wrapped around the hard chair back and squeezed until her knuckles turned white. Marian's life so far had been one of only predictable exchanges. She had done nothing out of the ordinary and nothing extraordinary had happened to her.

Katherine had changed that. Her very existence in the world made it a brighter, sharper place to Marian's eyes. Of course she was happy to see Katherine. But she was also overwhelmed. And maybe a little bit frightened.

Not frightened of Katherine, obviously. Frightened of her own heart, of the unknown, and of what she was capable of doing. Or capable of being. The future stretched out in front of her as a completely blank slate. There were no patterns or expectations to follow here.

The only thing left to do tonight was to go to bed. To go to bed and wait for her love to come to her.

Chapter 10

Marian was halfway through the nightly ritual of five hundred brush strokes through her honey-blonde hair when a soft knock finally tapped against the wooden door. She was out of her seat and across the room before she remembered to breathe. Marian rested her hand against the door and pulled in a calming breath, then another, before opening the door just wide enough to look into the hall.

Just as she imagined, Katherine was on the other side. Katherine's smile was small but full of genuine warmth. "Are you going to let me in?" she whispered.

Marian tugged the door open more widely and stepped to the side. Katherine ducked in with only a quick glance behind her.

"No one would think it scandalous for me to be in your room so soon after dinner, but I didn't want to take any chances." Katherine's smile spread and it was all Marian could do to keep herself from closing the distance between them. She did step closer, just a small, wavering step.

"I was afraid you wouldn't be able to find me." That wasn't the greatest of Marian's fears, but she couldn't tell Katherine that she was afraid she had been abandoned. That Katherine no longer wanted her in Kent, or in her life. That the certainty she felt at dinner about Katherine's feelings had waned as she waited.

"The hotel's not that big. A little thing like that wouldn't keep me away from you." Katherine's smile went from warm and comforting to positively mischievous. "Besides, I may have bribed the young man at reception."

"Katherine!" Bribery sounded bad but Katherine's desire to be with her, to find Marian and reunite with her, burned warm in her chest.

"Bribe isn't the right word. I just smiled and batted my eyelashes at him a bit." Katherine demonstrated the technique used on the desk clerk and Marian could easily see why he broke the rules. "And he let me know in which room my dear friend Lady Marian Fielding was staying so that I could check on her and make sure she was not feeling too poorly." Katherine laughed out loud. Her laugh was full of mirth and joy for life. That may have been the thing that drew Marian to her the most.

Despite loving this about Katherine, Marian felt the need to be the responsible one. It was so ingrained in Marian to be calm, to be sensible, and Katherine made her want to toss all that to the side. "Still, it was a risk. He could have refused to tell you, or he could tell someone you're here."

Katherine stepped forward, close enough that Marian's first instinct was to step back. That was immediately followed by the need to step forward again, into Katherine's arms. She did neither. Marian pushed down years of expectation and social nicety to stay close to Katherine. Katherine's arms came up and her hands gently cupped Marian's elbows.

"No one will know. And it's not as if I'm a man sneaking into your room."

"Isn't it?" Marian was breathless and bold. She inched forward until she could feel Katherine's heat seeping into her nightdress.

Katherine's smile was as untamed and brilliant as ever. "No, not really. Women like you and I are able to get away with so much more than men who prefer their own sex. Society looks at us and sees two women in want of a man, and then eventually two old maids to be pitied. Not something devious or perverse."

Marian could see it then. She and Katherine biding their time until the marriage market had passed them by and they were left to their own devices. It all seemed far too passive, too domestic, to be something Katherine would want.

"Is that what you see in our future?"

"Yes, if that's what you want. I thought by coming here..." The point of Katherine's tongue darted out across her lips. "That you wanted the same things I did."

In truth, Marian wasn't entirely sure what she wanted. Or if it was the same as what Katherine wanted. It seemed mired in uncertainty. They still stood so close together. It was hard to think. Marian's body swayed forward, just a fraction of an inch, to bring the tight points of her breasts to Katherine's chest. There was a slight pressure on her elbows where Katherine's hands rested. That pressure held Marian tight against Katherine's chest.

"I want to be with you." It's the truth as specifically as Marian could say. The warm weight of Katherine pressed against her was the closest to ecstasy she had ever felt. Katherine's puckish grin and clear blue eyes pulled at more than just the physical in Marian. Their conversations, their shared laughter, their silent times together. It all added up to what Marian wanted her life to be from this moment forward.

Katherine's hands rubbed along the back of Marian's arms, her fingers dipping under the short sleeves of Marian's summertime nightdress. Marian never considered this stretch of skin particularly sensitive, but tiny sparks ignited in the wake of Katherine's palms. It was a warm tingle that seemed to spread across her skin as Katherine stretched up on her toes to bring her lips close to Marian's ear.

"Do you know what goes on between men and women in the bedroom?" Katherine's lips ghosted across the lobe of Marian's ear and along her jaw, but it was her breath that made Marian's knees tremble. The soft caress of it under her ear and through the soft wisps of hair along the back of her neck made a bolt of overwhelming sensation shoot through Marian's core. It started a dull ache between her legs that made her want to squeeze her thighs together and rock forward in Katherine's embrace.

"Yes," Marian answered breathlessly. It wasn't completely a lie. She had some idea what married men and women did together, or what men did with their mistresses, but she didn't know what that meant for herself and Katherine.

Katherine pulled back enough to arch a skeptical eyebrow at her.

Marian managed to huff out sigh. "I know some things. What is appropriate for an unmarried woman." She remembered Cecilia telling her of kissing Henry in the gardens when they could slip away from her chaperone. Of Henry touching her breasts through her gowns in the dark. "Maybe a bit more than is appropriate."

"That's my girl," Katherine laughed against Marian's throat, letting her lips drag a few scant inches across Marian's skin. Marian's eyes fluttered closed and she tilted her head back in an unconscious plea for more. Katherine did not disappoint. She kissed with short, dry presses of her lips across Marian's throat, up to the hinge of her jaw, and back to the shell of her ear. Katherine pressed up on her toes, bringing their chests even more tightly together. Marian's breasts ached and her cheeks burned with the knowledge of how quickly she was becoming wanton.

"Most men take their pleasure from their wives or mistresses with little thought to giving pleasure in return. Some don't realise women are as capable of sexual joy as they are, some don't care, and some just don't know how." Katherine's bold talk only further inflamed Marian's cheeks but she pressed herself more firmly against Katherine's warmth in response. "But women together do not have to be that way. We know what female bodies are like and what they can do. We can better enjoy each other's company than the company of men."

"I'm not sure I know how to do that," Marian paused, licked her dry, rough lips. "But I would very much like to kiss you again." She could not raise her voice above a whisper. She felt Katherine's breath hitch against her throat.

"Yes, oh yes."

One of the hands that had been drawing tiny circles against the back of Marian's arm withdrew, only to cup the back of her head and tilt her face forward. She looked down into Katherine's eyes, into her blinding smile, and felt any lasting nervousness fade into the much more welcome butterflies of anticipation. There was nothing beyond this room. They were together, and though Marian could not fully see over the precipice Katherine was asking her to leap from, she would do so willingly and gladly.

Marian stayed stock-still, paralyzed except for her breathing, as Katherine brought their lips together. Marian felt the heat spread from that point of connection up across her cheeks and down the column of her throat. That burning flush settled across her chest as Katherine tilted her head so they fit more securely together.

It was a wash of sensation for Marian: the heat and pressure of Katherine's lips on her own, the tingles of feeling where Katherine's fingers dug into the tender flesh of her arm, the gentle scrape of her breasts against the inside of her nightdress. All of it only made her want to sway into Katherine more fully. To be in even closer contact with her even though they were already pressed together from thighs to lips.

Katherine tilted again and Marian felt the slick heat of Katherine's tongue slide across the seam of her closed lips. Her lips parted in response and Katherine smiled against her mouth just before her tongue dipped inside.

Marian wasn't prepared for this. Katherine had kissed her in the French style before, but this was different. Previously, it had been a shock. Now it was a promise. Katherine was precise and sweet, her tongue sweeping inside Marian's mouth and rubbing along Marian's own.

That movement loosened something in Marian. It felt as if liquid fire, something dark and heavy and molten, was sliding through her and settling between her legs in a deep ache. She swayed forward at that, unable to keep her body still a moment longer. Her hips pressed against Katherine's and their kiss deepened. Marian stroked her tongue along Katherine's, trying to parrot back the movements that had brought her so much pleasure just a moment ago. She needed to be closer, to get closer to Katherine, no matter what. Marian's arms wrapped around Katherine's shoulders and she pressed more firmly into the kiss. Marian lacked Katherine's finesse and grace when it came to kissing but she could not bring herself to care. Her lips moved against Katherine's and that liquid fire was only growing and becoming more demanding.

Katherine started to pull back, but Marian held her close and chased her tongue until she ended up sliding past Katherine's lips into another deep kiss. Marian was truly following only her instincts now. She was on a path she had only the faintest notions of before, and even then only with the picture of some vague future husband in mind. It was exhilarating that her body wanted these things, that it knew how to do this on its own.

Then Katherine moaned. There was no other word for the noise that sounded as if it was torn from deep within Katherine's chest. It was unladylike and bone-rattlingly erotic. It made Marian's nipples tighten against her nightdress and an answering whimper catch in her throat. To know she was affecting Katherine so, Katherine who was beautiful and knowledgeable and a wonder all on her own, was the most potent aphrodisiac Marian had come across yet.

Katherine pulled back again and Marian was too shocked, too caught up in what her own body was feeling, to stop her.

"I could kiss you until sun up. I just might." Katherine's lips were swollen red and slick.

I did that, Marian thought with a jolt of lustful pride. She had left her mark on Katherine.

Katherine looked up at her as if she hung the moon. Marian was not sure what to say; words had never been her strongest suit. Instead she dipped down and pressed her lips to Katherine's in another chaste kiss. Her heart still raced from the deeper kissing they'd just enjoyed, and Marian would have liked nothing more than to do that until dawn, but she was still too uncertain to initiate something so intense on her own. "You could. I have no objection."

Katherine's hands settled on Marian's hips with a strong squeeze that made Marian's knees wobble. "Is anyone going to come looking for you tonight?"

Marian shook her head. "No, I've already dismissed the maid who helped me dress for bed and my father wouldn't come for me unless it was an emergency."

"Good. There will be plenty more kisses, love. Plenty, I promise. But you're giving me a crick in my neck."

Marian laughed at that and leaned her head against Katherine's shoulder. It was comforting and intimate and allowed her racing heart to calm a few beats. "I have always been unfashionably tall."

"Nonsense. You are the perfect height."

"For reaching tall shelves?" She was shocked at how easily conversation came to her with Katherine, how easy it was to joke with her, especially in light of the taste of Katherine still against her tongue.

Katherine laughed, her warm breath sending a sensuous chill across Marian's neck. "That is a definite advantage, I can't lie. But I was thinking more for this." Katherine turned her head and laid light kisses against the side of Marian's throat.

It felt nice. Not as shockingly erotic as their earlier kisses, but intimate. Instead of sending a blaze of lust through Marian, it served to stoke the fire that was already there. Marian turned her head to give Katherine better access to her throat.

The kisses became bolder. They were longer than just a simple press of lips, and Katherine's tongue darted out to lick along Marian's skin. She kissed all the way down to the juncture of Marian's shoulder. Katherine pulled at the neck of her nightdress to expose more skin to the stuffy air of the hotel room only to quickly cover that skin with her lips and tongue.

Katherine sucked there, drawing the skin into her mouth and worrying it between slick lips. Marian felt the pull of Katherine's lips against her neck, but also in the tightness of her taut nipples and all the way through her core to that hot, wet place between her thighs. Everything Katherine had done to her this evening, all the kisses, the light caresses, all of it, led back to that place. Until now, Marian had never given her most intimate places a thought, but tonight they dominated her senses. She wanted to rock into Katherine, rock against her, and to rub herself against Katherine until that ache loosened.

Those kisses and nips continued across the front of Marian's throat. Katherine stretched the neck of her nightdress, pulling it so hard that it would never quite be the same again, so that she could play her lips and tongue along Marian's collar bone. Marian would have torn the dress to shreds right then and there if she were able. Her skin felt as if it were on fire.

A harder suck to the sensitive dip at the base of her throat caused Marian's back to bow. She pressed her flesh up to Katherine's lips like an offering and let out a cry. Marian's hands gripped hard to Katherine's shoulders to steady herself.

"Easy," Katherine murmured into the curve of her shoulder. "I'll take care of you. I promise." Katherine's hand slid upwards, burning a trail from Marian's hip to the swell of her breast. The thin fabric of the nightdress felt rough between them, but Marian did not know how to ask Katherine to remove it.

Katherine's fingers curled there, gently around Marian's breast. Her fingertips rested just shy of brushing the erect point of Marian's nipple. Marian wanted to press forward again and demand that Katherine touch her there. That was what Marian's body wanted to do, but the thought of wantonly seeking more pleasure made a furious blush stain her cheeks. She looked away instead.

Marian managed a handful of ragged breaths before she felt the pad of Katherine's thumb drag across the peak of her nipple. Marian whimpered watching that thumb pull back and forth. Her back arched and she pressed more firmly into Katherine's hand, unable to stop herself. The low light of the lamp and the shadows moving around them made the whole scene somewhat otherworldly. It was quickly becoming a world from which Marian would happily never return.

"That's it, my good girl. You like that?" Katherine looked down to also watch the play of her fingers across Marian's breast. "Not everyone does. And some like it more than others, so you'll have to tell me what you like."

Marian had to swallow a lump in her throat before she could speak. "Yes. I like it."

Katherine squeezed the flesh of Marian's breast in her hand. There was just enough to fit snugly in her palm. The light pressure on all sides of her breast, combined with the press of Katherine's thumb on her nipple, made Marian's breath catch.

Katherine smiled wickedly up at her and did it again, this time pinching and rolling Marian's nipple between her thumb and forefinger.

"Oh please. Katherine, please." Marian was not sure what she begged for, but she begged all the same.

Chapter 11

Katherine pulled Marian down into another searing, deep kiss. Marian wasted no time in tangling her tongue with Katherine's, pushing back and forth between their mouths. Katherine's hand moved to her other breast, teasing the nipple and squeezing it in her palm as they kissed.

The tight buds of her nipples felt as if they were connected by a living spark to one another, and then to the juncture of her thighs. It made a triangle of throbbing sensation, washing over her in waves.

"I need you out of this dress." Katherine's voice was huskier now and her hands skimmed down the front of Marian's nightdress to rest on her stomach. How hands pressed lightly to a stomach could be erotic and intimate, Marian would never know, but she felt as if she were safe and desired all at once. "Turn around and I'll undo your buttons."

Marian turned, but it felt as if she were in a dream. She swept the curtain of her golden honey hair over one shoulder, as courteously as she would have for Alice to undo her buttons after a good night's sleep.

Though she could not see, Marian felt the small tug and then give of Katherine releasing the mother of pearl buttons along her back. This nightdress was older in style and had small iridescent buttons making a straight line to the level of Marian's waist. It was uncomfortable to sleep in, but pretty. Katherine undid every single one in slow and careful motions. Marian could have pulled the dress over her head after just a button or two had been undone, but she liked the feeling of Katherine's careful fingers undressing her. The sides of the dress fell open and her skin was revealed inch by inch. Marian felt exposed, vulnerable.

When the last button gave way, Katherine placed a fingertip at the base of Marian's neck and drew a slow, sensuous line along the divot of her spine. Katherine paused there before sliding her palm forward and cupping Marian's hip. The drag of Katherine's hand under the loose fabric of her nightdress was the current highlight in a night full of new sensations. She looked down and could see the silhouette of Katherine's fingers through the fabric, clinging to her where they gripped at the curve of her hip. Just that sight alone made Marian draw a deep breath. Her hips rolled forward, silently encouraging Katherine's hand to continue its slide down. Down to where the ache at her center had turned hot and needy.

Katherine pressed a kiss to the top of Marian's spine. She probably had to stand on tiptoe to reach it. "Shhh, we'll get there, love. I promise. None of the other guests have retired for the evening and I want to take my time with you. I've been waiting for you for so long."

I've been waiting for this my whole life and never knew it.

Those kisses continued. Katherine trailed them down Marian's spine, following the same path and lingering pace that her finger had a moment earlier. Marian rounded her back in encouragement. Her arms hung at her sides with hands fisted in the cotton of her nightdress. She gently pulled the fabric away at both sides, subtly trying to bare more flesh for Katherine's lips to explore. She had never felt so wanton, had never expected to silently beg someone to kiss her body.

Marian was panting by the time Katherine stretched up, her front pressed firmly to Marian's bare back, to suck at the juncture of Marian's neck and shoulder. The satin of Katherine's gown felt decadent against the warm and damp places her mouth had so recently anointed. The contrast between such inappropriately heated flesh and proper dinner attire brought another blush to Marian's cheeks.

That gentle suck at the base of Marian's neck transformed into Katherine licking a long, hot path up Marian's spine all the way to the roots of her hair. Nose buried in Marian's hair and hand gripped tight at Marian's hip, Katherine spoke. "You are so beautiful. Your skin practically shines in the darkness."

Marian tried to turn in Katherine's grasp, desperate to kiss her again.

Katherine held her fast. "Not yet. I haven't kissed you enough here yet."

Everywhere Katherine pressed her lips or laid her tongue or dragged the blunt edges of her teeth felt like a fire seeming to ignite. The hand at Marian's hip moved to slowly caress the skin of her stomach. It worked upward until it was cupping Marian's bare breast under her slumping nightdress. Katherine squeezed the globe of it in her palm and rubbed her thumb across the taut nipple in a torturous back-and-forth slide.

Marian bent her head forward to watch the movement through the gauzy curtain of her nightdress. This also gave Katherine better access to her neck, where she redirected her mouth. Each kiss caused Marian's nipples to pull even more tightly and each caress to her breast made wetness slide between her thighs. Marian let out breathless little moans every time Katherine let her mouth linger against her skin or paused to pinch at her nipple.

Katherine's other hand worked into Marian's dress and squeezed her other breast hard. Katherine's fingers were wet when they first circled the peak of Marian's nipple. She had licked them.

Marian's hips bucked forward, desperately searching for some relief but finding none. "Please, Katherine. Please!"

Katherine panted against Marian's shoulder, no longer in control enough to lay kisses there. Her body was pressed to Marian's from shoulder to knee. Both of Katherine's hands worked Marian's breasts in tandem, squeezing and pinching and rubbing, until Marian was nearly incoherent. It took all her concentration to remain upright and not lean too heavily on Katherine in fear of tumbling both of them to the floor.

Katherine's hands went still, each cupping a breast, and only her thumbs rubbed gently across the swollen tips of Marian's nipples.

"Here, when we're like this, you call me Kitty. Only here, it doesn't have to be for anyone else. But when I have you in my arms, I want to hear you call me Kitty."

Marian arched her back and let her head tip back to rest on Katherine's shoulder, which had the pleasant consequence of pushing her breasts more firmly into Katherine's palms. "Yes, Kitty. Kitty. Please."

This time it was Katherine's hips that jumped forward, pressing her more tightly to Marian's backside. "Oh, god, yes." Marian was rewarded with an awkward, deep kiss that ended with the two of them panting against each other's mouths.

Marian tried to turn again, but Katherine stopped her.

"Surely we can...do more if I am facing you." The shame Marian felt for asking for what she wanted was substantially less in the heat of desire than it would have been earlier in the evening, but it still made her uncomfortable to be so forward.

"Not necessarily," Katherine replied. Marian could barely see her smile, but the edge of it was wicked.

Katherine kept kissing Marian's jaw, the side of her neck, and even down to her shoulder where her nightdress had fallen forward to bare more creamy skin. While Marian was distracted by those kisses, Katherine's hand trailed down her side, skimming over Marian's sensitive flank and hip, until Katherine's fingers raked through the coarse curls above Marian's sex.

Marian's breath caught and she pulled back just enough to look at Katherine over her shoulder. Katherine's fingers stayed there, caressing down through Marian's curls again and again.

That caress was maddening. It was indecent and set Marian's flesh on fire. Marian stayed still for several long moments, allowing Katherine to stroke her just shy of her most intimate place.

"This all right?" Katherine asked.

Marian took a deep breath, counted slowly to three in her head, and then deliberately canted her hips forward, pushing herself against Katherine's palm. She stretched her center toward Katherine's gentle fingertips. "Yes."

Katherine pressed a dry kiss to the shell of her ear before sliding her hand lower. "You're wonderful. Spread your legs wider for me."

Marian complied without thought, shuffling her feet out to spread her thighs to Katherine's wandering hand.

That hand dipped even lower, palm pressing flat against Marian's mound and fingertips nudging their way across slick folds. Katherine's fingers coaxed and rubbed, pulling layers of sensation from Marian that she had not known existed. When Katherine's fingers played quickly over the hot and aching nub at her center, the tension Marian had been feeling knotted and twisted deep in her core.

Her head lolled on Katherine's shoulder and all she could manage were small whimpers and moans as she rocked against Katherine's hand. Katherine pressed kisses against her neck and murmured encouragements against her overheated skin. Marian's nightdress had fallen away from her chest, exposing her breasts to the humid air in her room. If she looked down, she could watch as Katherine's wrist disappeared beneath the fabric low against her belly.

Not being able to see, only to feel, what Katherine was doing drove Marian's passion higher. As did the words Katherine whispered to her.

"I'm going to lay you out across your bed and taste you. I want to touch you everywhere, with my hands, with my tongue, everywhere." Katherine paired the most inappropriate of Marian's imaginings, things she had not even considered could be done between people, with a forceful pressure against that most sensitive nub. Marian craved her touch there more than any place else and cried out when Katherine rubbed her fingers against that spot. Marian's hips bucked, trying to bring even more contact and more pleasure between Katherine and herself.

Katherine pulled her hand away and Marian watched it reemerge from under the cover of her nightdress and move away from her body. She whined and tried to turn in Katherine's arms as that hand disappeared from her view, but a gentle pinch to her nipple stopped her with an indrawn breath.

"Wait. I'm not abandoning you."

Marian turned enough so that she could see the smile on Katherine's lips and could not help but smile in return. Katherine raised her fingers to her lips and the tip of her pink tongue darted out to lick them. She gazed mischievously up at Marian as she sucked three slim, pale fingers into her mouth. She held them there for a moment as Marian watched, mesmerised by the little movements she imagined Katherine's tongue making.

Katherine popped those wet fingers from her lips and slid them back into Marian's dress, not stopping until they dragged across her folds and shot pleasure deep into her core again. "This will make it better. I swear. The moisture helps."

Marian was at a loss for how it could possibly get better, but she could not fault Katherine's reasoning.

She rode on waves of pleasure. Like floating on her back in the sea when she was young. Other times, when Katherine dipped into her body or pressed hard against her center, the waves lifted her high. Her stomach dropped to her toes. She was on the edge of falling over the wave, of being swept under a churning sea, of drowning. She rode waves of pleasure up and down until sweat trickled along her collar bones and her breasts ached. Marian wanted to fall, she would beg Katherine to let her fall and be swept away by the sea, if she could only find the words.

Katherine's hand kept working on her, spreading Marian's own wetness around. That sea-like rise and fall of pleasure kept washing through her. Marian's hips rolled in a constant counterpoint to Katherine's fingers. It was nearly too much, until Katherine stopped.

It gave Marian a moment to catch her breath, but only a moment. Katherine pushed her nightdress away from her hips, letting it pool on the floor around Marian's feet. She pulled Marian toward the bed and laid her out atop the coverlet. Marian lay with her knees hooked over the side of the bed. Katherine stroked down her thighs and carefully parted them. For a fleeting moment, Marian thought she should be embarrassed. But she wasn't. She wanted Katherine to see her. She rose up on her elbows. It was just enough that Marian could see Katherine sink to her knees, framed between Marian's thighs.

"Lie back, my sweet."

Marian's mind filled with Katherine's voice from earlier. *Lay you out across your bed and taste you.* She couldn't respond in words. Instead, she gave a firm shake of her head and stayed perched on her wobbly elbows.

Katherine laughed at her, low and sultry and positively toe-curling, before leaning forward. Marian felt Katherine's hot breath against her center before anything else. In that brief, silent pause, it was all Marian could do to keep herself from arching upward and pushing her sex against Katherine's mouth.

Katherine came to her. That quick tongue darted out and flicked across the nub at Marian's center, setting Marian on fire. Katherine's tongue dipped through her folds, working into her and then back up again to spread wetness across the whole of Marian's sex. The assault on her center was too much. Katherine alternated fast and firm flicks of her tongue with gentle sucking. The more Marian writhed and the deeper her moans, the harder Katherine worked her.

"Kitty! Oh, Kitty. Please." Marian knew not what she begged for but she knew this was the end. This was the moment when the waves stopped catching her gently as she crested with them but instead bowled her over and under and tossed her as they wished. She was ready. She was ready to completely give over and be taken by the sea. To be taken by the pleasure Katherine was building inside her. If this was depraved hedonism, Marian wanted nothing else. For the rest of her life, she would want nothing else. She was sure of it.

Her back bowed, pulling her off the bed, and she fisted a hand in Katherine's dark hair. She shook and moaned, all her muscles going taut and staying that way longer than Marian ever thought was possible. Katherine had to grab hold of her bottom to keep Marian pressed against her mouth.

Katherine held her there, licking and sucking, until Marian stopped thrashing against the sheets and her muscles relaxed. She melted into a warm pool. Katherine kept licking, more gently and with the obvious intent to soothe rather than raise passion. Marian could feel desire stirring deep inside her again, as if one glorious completion would not be enough. Maybe she would never have enough of Katherine. That thought should have frightened her, would have frightened her just a few days ago, but instead it made her smile and think of the nights of passion stretched out before them. Katherine slowed her attentions, then stopped completely before crawling up the length of Marian's body. Her fine silks and satins pressed against the cooling sweat on Marian's flank made Marian feel even more debauched.

Katherine's face was flushed and her lips swollen and wet. She bent and kissed Marian deeply. Marian tasted the musky flavour of her sex on Katherine's tongue. She moaned into Katherine's mouth thinking of it, and wondering what Katherine herself would taste like. Her arms felt limp and her abdominal muscles ached, but laughter bubbled up in Marian's throat. She laughed quietly but uncontrollably, with tears welling in her eyes. Katherine let her laugh, pressing dry kisses to her wet cheeks until Marian spent herself.

After her laughter stopped, Marian raised herself up on shaky elbows to look down at Katherine reclining on the bed. She bent down and kissed Katherine deeply, trying to let enthusiasm and the depth of her feeling make up for the differences in their experiences. Marian was sure Katherine would understand. She knew Marian had never done anything like this before and yet she came to Marian anyway.

Marian pulled back and dragged her lips to Katherine's neck. "You. I want to do that to you. Tell me how?" she whispered against Katherine's flushed skin. There was something shocking and exciting about asking Katherine to instruct her in the art of love making.

Instead of answering with the hungry kisses and passionate touches Marian expected, Katherine groaned and sat up. "I should have changed into my nightdress and dressing gown before I came down here. We'll never be able to get this off and back on again and make me look decent. If anyone saw me sneaking down the hall disheveled…" Katherine stopped to look down at the dark, damp spots on her gown where Marian had rested against her. "Well, more disheveled anyway."

Marian sat up as well, pulling her arms around her bare breasts to cover them. "So, I can't…?"

"Oh, darling, my love. No, no, no." Katherine leaned over and kissed Marian again, coaxing her out of her lapse into self-doubt. "Just not tonight. It's my fault. I didn't plan it as well as I should have. I was too anxious to get to you."

"You would have sneaked down here in your nightdress? You can't wander the halls of a hotel in your dressing gown."

"I would sneak down here stark naked if I could." Katherine gave her an impish grin, the dimple on her cheek standing out proudly.

She reached up to caress Katherine's cheek. Katherine turned into it, placing a kiss against her palm. "I think even your father would take issue with that, not to mention mine."

"I would just have to calmly explain that I was on my way to ravish Lady Marian Fielding and couldn't possibly be overdressed for the occasion. It would be a scandal!" Katherine dissolved into giggles against Marian's shoulder. Marian wanted to reprimand Katherine for being so flippant about something as serious as their reputations, but she could not. She was too filled with love and joy to feel anything other than an exasperated fondness. Katherine's laughter died away before she spoke again. "I should go back to my room before the men retire for the evening and my father comes to check on me."

They kissed a few more times as Katherine helped Marian back into her nightdress and tucked her under the covers. The evening left Marian languorous and she melted against the mattress. The room felt much cooler now than it had when she was caught up in passion. She hugged the blanket to her shoulders.

Katherine kissed her again, against her brow, before turning to leave.

"Kitty?" Marian pulled her chin from under the duvet so she could look at Katherine's silhouette against the low lamp light. "I'll breakfast in the main dining room tomorrow. Perhaps you'll be there too? And after breakfast we could take a walk together?"

Katherine smiled widely. Marian could see it even in the dimness of the room. "I'd like that. I'll see you in the morning."

Marian was already slipping into sleep when Katherine closed the door behind herself.

Chapter 12

Katherine managed to meet Marian for breakfast the next morning, even if Katherine was so late that the coffee she requested from the waitress must surely be cold. Katherine sat beside Marian at the mostly empty table. Marian's skeptical eye must have been all too noticeable because Katherine gave her a cheeky grin before tearing away a piece of Marian's buttered toast and popping a too-large chunk into her mouth.

"What? I had a late night. Had terrible trouble sleeping. Seemed like I was all worked up over something and couldn't get my mind to settle."

Marian felt her cheeks heat and ducked over her tea cup to hide her blush. "Maybe you should mind what you do just before bed. Try to engaging in relaxing activities to better still your mind." She loved this boldness Katherine created in her, even when they were sitting, fully clothed, in a public dining room.

Katherine let out a loud bark of laughter, drawing irritated glares from a group of stout matrons a few empty seats away. "That's one of the things I like most about you, Marian. You're witty. I don't think most people realise that about you."

She couldn't help but chuckle at that. "I think you're forgetting my other positive qualities, like my manners, tact, and the decorum our families hoped I would pass on to you."

"Not a chance."

"No, I didn't think so."

Katherine smiled at the waitress as she dropped off a plate of kippers, toast, and eggs. She chomped on another piece of toast, smearing her fingers with melted butter. "Besides, I prefer some of your less refined characteristics." She dropped her voice low and leaned toward Marian. "Like the noises you make when I touch you." Katherine reached over to gently touch Marian's wrist. It was casual enough that anyone at the table might think they were just two young ladies sharing a confidence. Katherine pulled back quickly. "But most importantly, your capacities for affection and kindness."

Marian could not help but beam at her.

After that, breakfast went smoothly, even if their bent heads and laughter drew the matrons' eyes more than once.

❋ ❋ ❋ ❋ ❋ ❋ ❋ ❋ ❋ ❋

During the rest of the week, they met a little later than Marian would have liked but definitely earlier than Katherine was accustomed to, and ate breakfast together. Sometimes, their fathers joined them. Mr. Fuller would smile at them, obviously happy Katherine had made a friend, while Lord Denbigh ignored the young ladies all together. The men talked over the business of their day while Marian and Katherine plotted their daily escape.

They walked together in the mid-morning. Long walks through the town to the grassy hills beyond where they sat together in the shade of large trees and talked or read. The best moments were when they could be silent but still happy together. Marian had never felt contentment like the warm sun on her cheeks and Katherine's hand drawing lazy circles against the small of her back as she read. The morning would slip to afternoon before they returned to the hotel.

Evenings were a slow burn into pleasure and education. Dinner was taken in the formal dining room with the other hotel guests and, on two occasions, in a private dining room with just their fathers and Cecilia and Henry, who came to discuss business matters. Those nights were both a blessing and a curse. Marian was pleased to be in the smaller dining room, away from strangers and their judgmental gazes when Katherine laughed a little too loudly or leaned a little too closely, but when Cecilia was with them they were more restrained in their conversation. The after dinner rituals took longer as well. Marian was not unhappy to see her sister but she could not share her own happiness with the recently wed Cecilia, even though they were both glowing with new love and the discovery of passion. The secret weighed on Marian, but not as heavily as she had feared. It felt as if their secret were a precious thing between just Katherine and Marian, like one of the flowers Katherine still drew for her. Something brave enough to bud at the first sign of spring. Something to be protected and cherished. It warmed her and made her feel alive in a completely new way. That no one else would ever know dimmed her joy only slightly.

The nights were even more invigorating than the knowledge of that closely held, shared secret.

Katherine snuck into Marian's room every night, without fail, after they spent what felt like an inordinately long time in the hotel salon with the other ladies in residence. Over tea or sometimes a sip of sherry, the ladies talked of things Marian could never remember. She tolerated the conversation with a politely frozen smile on her face, but thought only of the warmth of Katherine's arms around her and the pleasure of Katherine's kisses against her lips. As well as down the length of her body.

Katherine always came to her with her hair down and in nothing more than her nightdress and dressing gown. Marian had no idea how she managed to sneak through the hotel without anyone catching her. Marian had laughed, had begged her to wear something else, but each night she came as if she were retiring for the evening. Her slippered feet were quiet on the planks of the hall and only the quiet *snick* of the unlocked door handle could be heard when she came to Marian. Unfortunately, Marian could not be said to have the same gift of silence in their time together.

The third night Katherine came to her, Marian nearly gave them away. Katherine was poised over Marian, weight resting on her elbows, so that they were aligned in a way that brought them together from their collarbones all the way down. Katherine, being several inches shorter, had to wriggle a bit to get in the best position. That wiggle caused Marian to moan, deep and loud from the back of her throat. Their breasts were pressed together and Katherine's movements brought the wetness of their sexes nearly together. Not quite, but oh so close. Marian rocked her hips up without realising what she was doing, aching for that contact.

She was met with Katherine's cheekiest grin.

"This is a thing that women do together," Katherine said as she rolled her hips down, rocking against Marian with delightful pressure, but still not quite where Marian ached for her.

Marian bucked upward and grasped on to Katherine's bottom to pull her closer. "This?"

"Yes, that's it exactly." Katherine rewarded her with another cant and drag of her hips. "Do you like it?"

In place of an answer, Marian jerked up to sear a kiss against Katherine's lips. She pushed her tongue deep in Katherine's mouth, as she had learned Katherine preferred, and was greeted with a moan in response. She lifted her hips up as high as she could to grind strongly against Katherine's sex. "Yes. I like it very much."

They rocked together for several long moments, sweat building up between their bodies, but never quite rubbing against that aching nub Marian longed to have touched. It was an exquisite torture that built a flame of desire inside Marian.

Katherine let her suffer like that, getting close to the pleasure she needed without actually reaching it, until Marian was whimpering beneath her.

"Here. It's better like this." Katherine shifted so that she straddled Marian's sweat-damp thigh and could grind her own leg against the heat of Marian's center. The change in sensation was instantaneous. It went from a tease that demanded Marian's body thrust up in search of release to a promise that if she ground down, pressed deep and hard against Katherine's thigh, she would find pleasure.

Marian grasped at Katherine's shoulders, her bottom, pinched the peaks of her breasts, touched her anywhere she could reach as the roll of Katherine's hips and press of Katherine's leg drove her wild. It was a much more vigorous affair than they had had before. Their lovemaking the previous two nights had been slow and gentle but this felt as if Katherine were trying to press her straight into that mattress and Marian had to push back against it to keep herself from being swallowed up. That give and take, the power and effort Marian could feel straining her muscles, was intoxicating. She teetered on the edge of pleasure, feeling both powerful and vulnerable as she exerted her strength on Katherine, against Katherine, to get what she needed.

Katherine was not unaffected either. "Oh, god, Marian. This is so good. You're going to come apart against me and I'm going to feel it." She shook in Marian's arms, lips against Marian's neck. Katherine licked the sweat away as it trickled to Marian's collarbone.

"Yes, I want to feel it too, Kitty. Please, let me feel it." Pride bloomed in Marian's chest. She was bringing this pleasure, this heady loss of control, to her lover. It was hers to gift and Katherine's to take. It was a shared power between them.

Marian acted on instinct alone. Some of the lessons Katherine had taught her flashed through her mind, but most were lost to the overwhelming sensations she was feeling. Her body wanted to flip them, to crawl over Katherine, and to be the one to ride her lover like this.

It was with those thoughts that Marian fell over the crest into her own release. It wasn't the slow, rolling wave-like pleasure of before. It was a roaring blaze from deep within her core, radiating outward until all her limbs were shaking. It was hard and fast and Marian could not control the way her body bowed and bucked against Katherine.

It wasn't until Katherine clamped a hand over her mouth that Marian realised she was crying out in pleasure. Keening as she found her release against Katherine's yielding body.

"Marian, shhhhh. You have to keep quiet. I'm here. I'm here." Katherine held her, pressing her thigh deeply to Marian's sex and letting her continue to rut against it. Marian bit hard against Katherine's palm. She could not stop the noises of pleasure entirely, they were being ripped from her chest without her say so, but Katherine gave her the means to control them as best she could.

It felt like a long time passed before that fire burned itself out, leaving Marian a shaking and limp mess against her sheets. Her fingers twitched with the desire to hold Katherine, either in the sweet way they had done before or to help her find her own release, but all Marian could do was slowly lift her arms and rest her hands against Katherine's hips. Those hips still rolled against her, rocking into her while Katherine panted and moaned against her neck.

Katherine pulled away from her, sitting up and looking like a goddess in the low lamp light. Naked and glowing with the peaks of her larger breasts standing out in shadow. She glowed rosy pink with a sheen of perspiration. "Marian, I need. I need something else."

Marian was exhausted but she would not deny Katherine. She squeezed lightly at Katherine's hips. "Anything, Kitty."

She was given a scorching kiss and one last roll of Katherine's hips, which dragged the hot, damp skin of Katherine's center across her thigh, before Katherine clambered up her body, settling her knees next to Marian's ears. Marian's hands rose to cup Katherine's bottom automatically as Katherine lowered herself down, bringing her wet sex to Marian's lips.

Marian's tongue shot out, caressing and rubbing along Katherine's labia all the way up to the nub at her center. From this angle, Marian could watch as Katherine used one hand to brace herself on the headboard and the other to pinch her own nipple. Her hips rolled back and forth in the same way they had moved against Marian's thigh. It was a slower rhythm this time as Katherine and Marian worked their bodies, mouth and hips, together to pleasure Katherine.

This wasn't the first time Marian had made Katherine come with her mouth, but it was the first in this position. Marian liked it. She liked the feeling of being at Katherine's mercy even as she was the one giving pleasure. Katherine was taking it from her as readily as she was giving it. She had the perfect view up the long line of Katherine's body to watch as Katherine enjoyed herself.

It wasn't long before that gentle rocking motion grew faster, harder and Katherine was biting her own lip to keep from crying out. Katherine held there for a moment. Her hips stopped rocking and Marian surged up to keep her tongue and lips in contact until the final tremors of pleasure passed. It was only a moment before Katherine lowered her exhausted body down, settling tucked next to Marian's.

"Do you think anyone heard us?" Marian asked as she stroked Katherine's hair. Her lips and tongue were slick with the taste of Katherine and though the fear of discovery was ever present, it was significantly harder to care about that when she had Katherine in her arms and she felt so very loved.

Katherine shrugged, her shoulder sliding against Marian's just enough to convey the gesture. "I don't know. Maybe. If they did, we'll just run away to Paris. How's that? Open a bakery or something. They don't mind our kind there."

It was still strange to Marian that such a kind existed and that she was part of it. Perhaps she had been part of it all along and just didn't realise until Katherine had opened her eyes.

"Can you even bake?"

"Not a scone."

"I think I see a fatal flaw in your plan."

Katherine kissed her then, sweetly and with gratitude and love. "We'll figure something out."

Chapter 13

They were ten days into Marian's stay in Kent, with Lord Denbigh giving no signs of returning to Warwick Paddox, when the Fieldings, the Cliffords, and the Fullers were invited to a ball.

Though the title "a ball" may have given the gathering too much credit. It was nothing compared to the soirees and dances Marian had attended during her Seasons in London. It was more like a glorified dinner party with some musicians and a small dance floor. Katherine seemed charmed though. She appreciated any excuse for a party. And Cecilia was happy to be out in company as Mrs. Clifford. Marian had never been comfortable with the crowds at balls in London but this more intimate setting among the wealthy families in Kent was more to her taste.

When the dancing started, Marian took a turn with a few young men but Katherine was the real star of the show. Marian heard her laugh and caught glimpses of the deep blue of her gown as she twirled past. Even in passing, she was radiant. The room seemed more energetic, the music louder, just for having her there. They had sat next to each other at dinner and Katherine had secreted a hand onto her thigh for most of the pudding course. Marian felt no jealousy or unease. Let her have fun dancing with the gentlemen, because Marian knew whose arms she would be in come the dark of night.

As the night wore on, Marian's caught the sound of Katherine's laughter more and more, and at louder and louder volumes. Others were starting to notice it as well. Marian saw the crowd searching Katherine out, including Lord Denbigh himself. He watched Katherine laugh too loudly and stand too close to a group of young men. They had been paying attention to Katherine all night. Marian had noticed these men as well but paid them no mind, but now she saw them as the others in the room saw them. As predatory and leading Katherine to impropriety. What the well-to-do of Kent didn't know was that Katherine didn't need to be lead very far to reach impropriety. She practically revelled in it before meeting Marian. Even now that they had formed an understanding, Katherine still enjoyed impropriety. Just now with more focus. And more discretion.

For Marian's father to see that behaviour again now could be disastrous. She trusted Katherine not to do truly anything awful but Marian also knew Katherine would skirt the line of impropriety as closely as she could.

And the volume of her laughter was starting to concern Marian.

Marian watched her father's brows draw together as Katherine leaned closer to one particular gentleman so he could say something into her ear. Lord Denbigh frowned in Katherine's direction before turning back to the conversation he'd been having with Mr. Fuller. Marian had lost the thread of her own conversation while she watched Katherine's increasing brazenness and her admirers' reactions to it. Trying to watch Katherine, Lord Denbigh, and participate in conversation was too much. As soon as an opportunity arose to excuse herself from the conversation, she made her way to Katherine.

Katherine gave her a grin that spread from ear to ear when Marian joined her circle of acquaintances, but did not say anything. For a moment, Marian feared Katherine would reach out and take her hand or pull her close by the hips as they often did in private.

Katherine's expression held the same sort of longing Marian often saw when they were alone. It was dangerous in public.

Joining a conversation already in progress, especially one so boisterous, would have intimidated Marian before Katherine had come along. She was changed now. In some ways, those changes were undeniably good. Other changes would not be seen as positive by society, but that was something Marian was more than willing to live with. She just had to make sure Katherine kept their secret as long as possible. The first step to that was not drawing any unnecessary attention to herself with bad behaviour.

Marian stayed quiet, listening and watching Katherine, until there was as suitable lull in the conversation.

"Miss Fuller, would you take a turn in the gardens with me? I'm feeling a bit overheated." Marian tugged firmly on Katherine's arm. Katherine's eyes were glassy and her skin flushed. Marian needed to get her attention and hold it.

"I thought we were supposed to take a turn about the room if we have secrets to tell," Katherine quipped back, standing firm.

"No secrets, just a bit of fresh air." Marian needed to get her out of there.

Katherine graced her with another sweet smile. "I'm sorry gentlemen, but my very good friend, Lady Marian, requires my presence." There was a bit of uproar from the men gathered around her. "Oh, don't worry! I'll be back in time for the next round of dancing!" That was met with a cheer more suited to a dance hall than a ballroom as Katherine pulled Marian toward a set of large French doors that led to the gardens.

She hooked her arm in Marian's and walked them past the rose bushes to the other side of a tall hedgerow. Once they were hidden from view, Katherine leaned over and stole a kiss. Marian wavered toward her, leaning into that familiar comfort, before jumping back and dropping Katherine's arm.

"Katherine!" she hissed. "Someone could see."

"No one will come looking for us. Your father probably thinks you dragged me out here for a stern talking-to." Katherine's breath puffed out on a cloud of heavily whiskey scented air.

Marian was shocked. "Have you been drinking strong spirits?" The ball wasn't serving anything stronger than punch in the public rooms but Marian hadn't been watching Katherine that closely. Maybe the men were being served spirits away from the women and Katherine had managed to get herself a tumbler.

"It's just some whiskey. Your liquor is terrible here, in case you didn't know. American spirits are far superior." Katherine happily propped her leg up on a convenient stone bench and pulled her skirts up all the way to her knee before fishing underneath to pull a silver flask from a beneath a garter on the outside of her leg. "Of course I have to wait until the maid thinks she has me all dressed to go out before adding this last accessory, but it's well worth it."

"Kitty…" Marian couldn't keep the disappointment from her voice.

"Oh no, you don't get to call me that when I know you're angry at me. I wanted you to call me that all the time and you wouldn't, so now it's just for between us. When we're alone and things are good." Katherine tipped back the flask and took a swig, but the flask came up empty.

Marian tried a different tactic. "It's just that I thought you weren't going to do this anymore."

"I hate balls."

"You loved the balls you spoke of in New York."

Katherine scoffed. "Those are not like this, and you know it."

"I suppose not. I thought you would like this too. You always seem so energetic and ready to talk to people."

"No. I like talking to people but not like this. No one wants to talk to me about the things that actually interest me." Katherine slumped down to sit in the middle of the bench. "You're the only one who thought I was more than just a silly American girl. You're the only one that listened to me."

Marian wanted to scold Katherine. She needed a stern talking-to. But she looked miserable. Instead, Marian sat down, gingerly perching next to Katherine, afraid that she might bolt. "That's because I love you."

"No. You listened even before you loved me."

Marian laughed at that and risked twining her fingers with Katherine's, letting them come to rest on the dark blue satin of Katherine's lap. "I don't even remember when that was. Before I loved you, I mean."

They sat silently. It was calming just being together in the garden. The air was warm and the night pleasant but it did nothing to ease the tension between them.

Katherine finally spoke up. "I can't be who people expect me to be here without the stronger spirits. Punch or wine isn't enough. It's the only way I'm able to really relax when there's a room full of men that want to dance or flirt with me or when I have to uphold my father's expectations. Or your father's."

Upholding those expectations had always been easy for Marian. She was never outgoing, never wanted to talk about more than the weather or some innocuous society gossip with young men or the other young ladies waiting for a dancing partner. It didn't cut Marian to keep herself hidden the way it did Katherine.

She squeezed Katherine's palm. "What did you want to talk about with them?"

"Business."

"Business?" Marian was genuinely confused. She had heard Katherine discuss business matters over dinner with Mr. Fuller, much to Lord Denbigh's consternation, and Katherine seemed to know more than most daughters about her father's holdings and development plans. But that was a far cry from discussing business at a gathering of strangers.

Katherine was quiet again for a moment and Marian let her take her time. "I have a good head for business. Father talks through most of his acquisitions and schemes with me before he agrees to anything."

It was a shock. It was definitely out of the ordinary for a father to seek his daughter's counsel on financial matters, but she could see how Katherine's quick mind would excel at business. It also explained how Katherine was so sure that Lord Denbigh would travel to Kent, and how she knew about their fathers' plans with the factory here.

"If I had been born a man, I could have been excellent at business. Could have made a fortune. But instead, I'm reduced to conversations about the weather or music or plays and I just don't care about any of it."

Marian leaned against Katherine's shoulder. "If you had been born a man, I would not love you."

"Yes you would. I would have charmed you regardless of my sex." The light, smirking tone was not quite back in Katherine's voice but she sounded less melancholy.

Marian leaned in a bit harder, pressing their shoulders together. "I don't know. You've quite convinced me to the benefits of women. I don't think I would have responded as well to courting from a man, even if that man was you. The few overtures from young men during my seasons were never enough to turn my head."

"They simply weren't as charming as I am."

Marian lowered her voice. "Maybe I was waiting for you."

Katherine dipped her head so that it rested against Marian's shoulder. This was more intimate than Marian would ordinarily be comfortable with where they could be caught, but she could always claim Katherine was feeling ill if they were spotted. Maybe Katherine's behaviour in the ballroom could be explained as a touch of illness. The quick kiss Marian pressed to Katherine's forehead would have been harder to explain away, but Marian did not care. The dark of the garden would shield them. Even so, she did not let her lips linger.

"Do they have violets in this garden?" Katherine asked, with her head still resting on Marian's shoulder.

"I don't think so. Why?"

Katherine looked up and Marian could barely make out the blue of her eyes in the low light. "Because you should always have violets in your hair." She reached out and touched a few of the soft strands of hair at Marian's nape. She looked almost sad.

Faint strains of music started up in the ballroom once again.

"Father talked to me about this plan with your father. To buy factories in Kent and set Mr. Clifford up in business, then to expand with even more factories." Katherine paused and pulled away. Marian's instinct was to follow, to tug Katherine back to her and reassure her with warmth and affection. The music faded away again before Katherine spoke, "I told him not to do it."

That was even more shocking than Katherine's confession of a passing interest in business affairs. "Told him not to? Why?"

Katherine paused. Insects chirped and buzzed around them, seeming louder than the musicians had been. She took a deep breath before speaking again. "Because it's not going to work."

Marian knew little of her father's plans for Henry's establishment in business. Despite the Fielding's recent financial troubles, or maybe because of them, her father did not speak about financial affairs with the family. In fact, Marian could not remember when Lord Denbigh ever discussed or sought counsel from his family when it came to business investments or money. He'd been an active businessman her entire life and she had no idea what that really meant. She assumed this venture was simply to set Henry up so that he could take proper care of Cecilia after their marriage, especially if the Fielding's own fortunes were failing.

"Why won't it work?"

Katherine looked up at her, shocked. "You think I could be right?" Deep in her gut, Marian believed her. Katherine was clever and knew more about this whole situation than Marian did, but there was always a small kernel of doubt when facing the unknown.

"I don't know. I don't know the details of their venture, and you haven't told me why you think it's doomed to failure yet. But, I believe in you and I know how intelligent and perceptive you are."

Katherine graced Marian with a small smile before looking back to their folded hands resting in her lap. "This is the wrong place for it. There has been some interest in housing manufacturing and storage facilities in Kent, but it's limited. Your father, and mine, think that the great industrial towns in the North are failing. They are in a decline but that's to be expected so soon after the war. It won't last, they'll regroup and recover, and Kent will not grow to be some new manufacturing center of England and their investment will never turn a profit." It came out in one great stream of words, as if Katherine had been holding on to it for a very long time.

Marian's head spun. These simple, terse statements were more financial speculation than she had heard in her entire life. Coming from Katherine only made it stranger. She thought of what a failed business opportunity would mean for her father, and for Henry and Cecilia.

"If this plan fails, how bad will it be?" Marian asked quietly, afraid of what Katherine's answer might be.

"Marian, why do you think Lord Denbigh brought my father here from New York?"

"For his expertise?" Truly Marian was unsure. She had not considered it before.

Katherine let out a great sigh and pulled away from Marian. She rose and walked a few steps back out onto the gravel path. The sound of stones crunching under her slippers sounded in time with Marian's increasing heart beat.

"No. It was for the money." Katherine looked back at Marian, her gaze sorrowful and more troubled than Marian had ever seen. "The aristocracy is failing, Marian. Agricultural land barons aren't producing like they used to. Industrialisation means the money is going elsewhere. Going into business and investing wisely has made sure Warwick Paddox hangs on longer than most, but… it's only a matter of time until your father has nothing left, and a business disaster will make that happen sooner rather than later." Katherine jerked her head toward the ballroom. "You might as well get back in there and try to land a husband. It might be your last chance to be taken care of."

Marian was livid. More than livid, she was hurt and confused. "How can you say that to me? That's not what I want. Even before I met you, it wasn't what I wanted and now— you act like I don't know the world is changing. Everything has changed so fast, I'd have to be a fool to miss it." Marian forced herself to stop, to bite off the flow of words before she said something they both would regret.

"It's my fault. If I had been able to convince my father not to enter into this scheme with your family, you might not be facing ruin." Katherine was still somber, meeting Marian's rising anger with calm. She kept her face turned away from Marian.

It was ludicrous that Katherine would blame herself for any misfortune that might befall the Fieldings. The actions of their fathers were not in her power to control. The idea that Katherine would be able to talk men set on an idea away from it was laughable. Marian wanted to cry and stomp her feet. If this was the blame that was poisoning Katherine's heart to her, it should be easy to overcome. Marian should have seen that Katherine was uneasy, that she doubted the strength of their bond, before tonight.

"We are facing ruin anyway. I know our financial footing has been unsteady for awhile, I just didn't know how quickly things might change. It seems like there's no stopping it." Marian rose and moved slowly to Katherine's side. "You're not responsible for that. I'm sure you gave your father excellent counsel but he made his own decision. As did my father." Marian wrapped her arms around herself, considering what the future Katherine spoke of could mean. "If it goes poorly, then I'll have to deal with that. Regardless of marriage, I don't want to be taken care of by my father forever. I want to be self-sufficient."

"You don't have to be self-sufficient. Not entirely. We could do it together." Katherine was quiet and serious. Moreso than Marian had ever known her to be. She vibrated with restrained, nervous energy. That seriousness forced a smile from Marian. Katherine was always full of compliments and affection but this spoke of a deeper commitment. Maybe a lifetime.

"Make our own futures, but together?" It was what Katherine had said all along. They were independent women, both in spirit and likely soon in circumstances.

Katherine nodded. Marian could see the desire to say more on her face. Katherine was always the first to speak up, the first to push forward with a plan. Whether it was the whiskey or nerves that kept Katherine from speaking, Marian did not know. But she would have to be the one to find all the kind and reassuring words that needed to be said between them.

"That's what I want too. You don't take care of me. You support me and your care is in your affection, not in a desire to coddle or rule over me. We're equals." Marian crossed back to the bench, feeling Katherine's eyes on her the whole way. She carefully picked up the empty and abandoned flask before walking back to Katherine. "But you can't do this again. You can't hide behind strong drink."

Marian's anger still smouldered like a banked fire but other feelings also fought for dominance. Happiness at Katherine's desire to be with her forever, unease about her family's future, concern about Katherine's drinking. All of it stewed and stormed together.

"But I hate balls."

"I'll be with you from now on."

Katherine was quiet for a moment, considering the ground seriously. Her slippered feet scuffed the gravel back and forth. "That might not be enough." Katherine sounded quiet, almost child-like in her concern.

"Then we'll go somewhere we're not expected to go balls. If the upper class disappears, there won't be any more balls anyway."

"There will always be balls. You can't keep people from wanting to have a good time, and some of them think that's what this is."

"Maybe they'll be like the balls in New York, and not like this anymore."

"It will take a long time until those are the majority of social engagements." Katherine kicked at the earth again, sounding absolutely petulant.

Marian reached out and cupped her hand around Katherine's elbow. Katherine leaned into her arm instantly. "This is why people think you're impulsive and poorly mannered. This isn't the person you are when you're with me."

"I am impulsive and poorly mannered. You're just biased."

"You're... impish."

Katherine laughed. Still definitely not sober but she sounded much more like herself. Marian's heart jumped with hope. "Now I know you're biased."

"Puckish even."

"Aren't those the same thing?" Katherine's smile was warm and she caught Marian's hand in hers.

Marian could not help but smile back. "Not strictly speaking. There are some minor, but distinct, differences."

"I expect a complete recitation of those differences later." A hint of Katherine's normal impish, puckish grin curved her lips and Marian was so, so glad to see it genuinely return. She was so joyful that their fight seemed to be over she nearly missed the suggestion in Katherine's voice.

Just nearly. Instead it sent a warm jolt through her stomach. "We could claim you're not feeling well. Call the car to take us back to the hotel."

"I've faked headaches, and even female troubles, to get out of social engagements. I know how it's done." Katherine dropped Marian's hand but immediately faltered, twisting her fingers together in front of her stomach. Just when Marian thought they had made up and were again in agreement, she could tell there was something else Katherine needed to say. Marian gave her a few quiet moments to rally herself to say it.

"I told the men I was talking to that the plan wouldn't work."

That fell like a lead weight in Marian's gut. "What?"

Katherine looked up with eyes full of anguish. "Several of them are here tonight to talk about investing with our fathers. I told them not to. That moving manufacturing to Kent was a terrible idea. That it was doomed to fail."

Marian's heart beat faster in her chest. "Do you think any of them believed you?"

"Does it matter? If your father finds out, he'll think I tried to sabotage their financial arrangement on purpose. Or he'll just think I'm being spiteful. He'll be furious." Katherine's laugh was hollow and lifeless now.

That was something Marian hadn't considered. Despite Katherine's remorse, this could have all been intentional. She had to know for sure. "Was it deliberate sabotage? Are you trying to ruin us?" The 'us' put Marian firmly back into a camp with Lord Denbigh, and Henry, and Cecilia, and the rest of her family.

That did not go unnoticed by Katherine, who flinched away from Marian. "Of course not. I wouldn't do that to you. I don't want you to be destitute. Didn't I just say that? I want you to be happy. To be secure!" Katherine moved to rake a hand through her hair but jerked her arm back down at the last moment. "We were just talking and— and I can't keep my big mouth shut."

Marian took another step toward Katherine. "If they believed you…"

"I know, I know! I don't know how important they are to our fathers' plan but—" Katherine cut herself off to take a deep breath. "I know."

"You're right. My father will be furious."

"And are you?"

Marian took a moment to think about that, to breathe down the knee-jerk reaction of anger. The tumultuous whirlwind of emotions she had experienced tonight were exhausting. She could barely think. "I'm not pleased. But maybe, if you're convinced this will fail, ending it sooner rather than later will be a benefit."

Katherine gave her a weak smile. "I'm sorry. Truly I am. I'm rotten at self-control."

"That's not my favourite thing about you, you know."

"I know," Katherine whispered. "Can we call the car? I just want to go to bed." Katherine looked wrecked. Her shoulders slumped and her spine rounded, drained of confessions for tonight.

Marian gathered her strength. She wasn't happy with Katherine, but she knew it was up to her to get them out of this.

"Follow me inside, but stay away from crowds. I'll find Father and say I'm taking you back because you have a headache. Don't follow me when I talk to him. Stay back. He won't believe us but he won't care either. Just try not to draw any more attention to yourself, all right?"

Katherine nodded and, as meek as Marian had ever seen her, followed Marian to the house.

They barely made it inside before Lord Denbigh cornered them. Katherine had no time to get away. His shoulders were stiff and his neck flushed red in a way Marian knew had nothing to do with the heat of the ballroom. He stood dangerously close to Katherine. If they hadn't been in a crowded social setting, Marian thought he would have grabbed her by the arm.

"Foolish girl," Lord Denbigh seethed through gritted teeth. "What have you been telling people?"

"I told the truth. Your plan is flawed." Katherine never knew when to demure.

Marian tried to discreetly step between them. "Father-"

Lord Denbigh plowed right over Marian's protest. "What do you know about it, girl? You know nothing about finances or what we're building here. You spoke out of turn."

Katherine's anger was rising. Her cheeks were flushed and she clenched her fists at her side. She was gearing up for a fight and Marian had to get her out of there before someone said or did something regrettable. By now, Mr. Fuller had joined them and was hovering nervously behind Lord Denbigh.

"Father!" Marian was as loud as she could be without drawing more attention to them. She needed to redirect her father's attention to her, and away from Katherine. The clusters of attendees nearest to them were starting to notice the commotion.

Lord Denbigh turned to her, blinking as if seeing her there for the first time. It may have been the first time she had ever raised her voice to her father.

"Miss Fuller is not feeling well. I need to take her back to the hotel so she can get some rest. Please, call the car for us. You and Mr. Fuller can stay here and continue your conversations." *And try to undo the damage Katherine has done.*

It was the most assertive she had ever been with him. It wasn't comfortable for Marian. It wasn't in her nature to be outspoken, but for Katherine's sake she would do it. In truth, she felt a bit powerful standing up to her father. Powerful and frightened.

Lord Denbigh's anger did not seem abated, but rather like a banked fire. "Yes," he bit out. "I'll call the car. Get her out of here."

Chapter 14

After the car dropped them back at the hotel, Katherine followed Marian quietly to her room. The meekness worried Marian even more than the standoff with her father. Lord Denbigh's anger would fade in time.

When they were children, her father was always quicker to forgive some youthful mishap, a broken vase or an invasion into his study by overeager young girls, if she and Cecilia remained out of sight. Cowing Cecilia into the nursery for the rest of the day was likely a lot easier than convincing Katherine not to go looking for trouble again. Katherine invited trouble simply by existing. As sure as Katherine Fuller breathed, trouble would find her.

Just a few months ago, Marian would have stayed far away from a person like that. Now, it was exciting. But it would only remain *exciting* if she could keep Katherine from crossing her father again. Keeping Katherine with her was Marian's goal. Being separated by Lord Denbigh's anger, by his power over them, could not be allowed to happen. Not after they had decided their futures lay together.

Katherine collapsed in Marian's bed still wearing her evening gown. Pools of deep blue satin and lace trim spilled out across the hotel's white sheets. Katherine's eyes screwed tightly closed and her face pulled into a grimace.

"You need to change." Marian didn't want to toss Katherine from her rooms, but if she would go change now she could sneak back to Marian's before their fathers returned from the ball.

"Can't I borrow one of yours?"

Marian's nightdress would be comically long on Katherine. Long enough to trip her if she wasn't careful. Instead of protesting, Marian fished her extra nightdress from the wardrobe and placed it on the bed near Katherine's curled hands.

She turned her back and started to peel her own peach and cream silk dress away. When she reached the laces and stays she could not undo on her own, Katherine was there, unasked but welcome. Katherine undressed her in silence, until the final layers of fabric fell away. That was one definite benefit of going to bed with another woman: the need for a maid was greatly reduced.

Marian shifted away only enough to step into her nightdress. Katherine dutifully took up the buttons in the back.

There was a soothing comfort in being stripped bare by Katherine and in returning the favour without expectation. It was a different kind of intimacy than sex. It felt steadier. Katherine finished, pressed a kiss to Marian's shoulder and turned so Marian could help her undress.

"Have I ruined everything?" Katherine's voice was quiet and remorseful, sounding as if the lingering effects of drink had left her.

Marian sighed as she skimmed her fingertips up the line of buttons against Katherine's back. Marian took her time and Katherine let her work in silence, until Marian's fingers popped the last button free and she was ready to respond.

"No. Father will be angry for some time, so it's best if you stay out of his way. Your father didn't seem-"

"No, Marian, I meant between us."

Marian froze at that. It had never crossed her mind that Katherine's behaviour would ruin their relationship. She had been angry but never enough to consider this the end, or even the beginning of the end. Quite the opposite in fact.

"I don't think so." Marian chose her words carefully. "I'm upset. I don't like how you depend on strong drink when you're uncomfortable, and I don't like your behaviour when you're in your cups, but that doesn't mean you've ruined anything." She nudged Katherine's shoulders to get Katherine to turn round and tug the nightdress over her head. This was a conversation best had while both parties were in similar states of undress.

Katherine turned and stood still while Marian smoothed and settled the nightdress around her. Marian took up the buttons on the back this time. "This time. I do things like this all the time. You'll grow tired of it and chuck me."

It sounded like something that had happened before and Marian's heart ached for her.

"You won't do it all the time anymore. You have me." Marian finished her work on the buttons and bent to kiss Katherine's shoulder. She wrapped her arms around Katherine's middle and held her.

"I'm sure I'll still do it sometimes. And sometimes is too much."

Marian smiled a bit and kissed her again. "I know you will. A full reformation would be too much to hope for in any case. You'll work on it and I'll help you and that's the best we can do." She squeezed Katherine a bit tighter. "Coming here was my commitment to you. I plan to keep it. As long as you still want me to."

Katherine turned in Marian's embrace, raising her arms to loop them around Marian's neck. "Of course that's what I want. I just worry about wanting it to much."

Marian had never felt wanted, not like this, in her whole life, much less wanted *too much*. It was a heady thing to finally feel love and want coming from the beautiful woman in her arms. She loved Katherine, loved all of her, even the parts she didn't necessarily like all the time. The same impulsivity that led Katherine to smile up at her mischievously also led to the drinking and the talking out of turn. They could work together to tame it somewhat. Never completely though. She would not see Katherine broken and cowed.

She ducked to capture Katherine's lips. It was still usually Katherine that initiated this sort of intimacy but she melted against Marian. She still tasted of whiskey and it made Marian want to kiss her until all traces of it had been washed away.

The kiss was long and unhurried. It did not build up to a more immediate passion, but communicated comfort and devotion. They kissed like that for a long time, on the lips, across each other's cheeks and jaw, with their arms wrapped around each other and Katherine playing with the wisps of hair at Marian's nape.

"You should go back to your room soon," Marian managed to whisper against Katherine's cheek.

"I know. I don't want to, though. And besides, I'm already in my nightdress."

"You're in my nightdress, really."

Katherine chuckled. "Obviously. I would never be caught dead in something so old fashioned and demure."

Marian pinched her arm, just enough to sting. They smiled together and some of their regular ease returned. A reckless thought struck Marian. "Stay here. If we're found out, we can say that you were too ill to stay on your own last night. That I took care of you."

It was a good enough cover for spending the night together. Nothing that would work frequently but after Katherine's behaviour at the ball, it was believable.

"Your father won't be angry?"

Marian shrugged, stepping back from Katherine but taking her hand to pull her toward the bed. "Maybe. He'll think me naive for taking care of someone who brought her sore head and upset stomach on herself with overindulgence but I don't care about that. Stay with me."

Katherine hesitated. Marian pulled again. "Kitty, please."

Katherine's shoulders relaxed at the sound of her pet name on Marian's lips again. She walked forward and sat on the edge of the bed. Marian crawled in behind her, pulled her down under the covers, and arranged them so Marian was spooned behind her.

Katherine scooted and wriggled until they were both comfortable and the sheets began to heat beneath them. It took long, silent minutes until Katherine's breathing evened out and deepened in sleep. Only when that happened did Marian feel the tension release from her own body. Her shoulders slumped and her back relaxed enough that she could begin to slide into sleep as well. The tuck of their knees together and the warmth of Katherine's stomach under her arm was the greatest comfort Marian had felt since she had been held through the night by her own mother.

They had never spent the night together. Their time together was stolen in furtive snatches but never in just holding each other as they slept. It would be hard to give this up tomorrow.

✿✿✿✿✿✿✿✿✿✿

Breakfast the next morning was more than awkward. Marian left Katherine in her bed to continue sleeping. Katherine hadn't entirely escaped the lingering effects of her night of overindulgence, despite how sober she had seemed when they finally fell asleep. She had woken up with an aching and dizzy head.

It was better that Marian went to breakfast alone anyway. She needed to keep Katherine and Lord Denbigh apart, while presenting her best face to her father. An early breakfast without Katherine was the best way to do that.

Her father always rose early, even after a long night out, so Marian was sure to be there as dawn broke. She was exhausted, physically and emotionally, but was already seated with a full breakfast in front of her before Lord Denbigh and Mr. Fuller entered the breakfast room. The room was nearly deserted at this hour.

She picked delicately at a piece of toast until Lord Denbigh and Mr. Fuller took seats opposite her. Mr. Fuller looked nearly as tired as she felt. Marian gave her father a small smile that was not returned.

Lord Denbigh did not let more than a few bites pass Mr. Fuller's or Marian's lips before he started in on the root of their unease.

"Your daughter was inappropriate and that is going to cause us difficulties." This was said as a statement of fact, rather than an interpretation of the night's events. His jowls shook with anger.

Mr. Fuller was smart enough to recognize that an attempt to save face for himself or his daughter would be pointless. He nodded in agreement instead. "I will speak to Katherine about her behaviour. It will not happen again."

"You should send her away. Put her on a steamer back to New York as quick as you can." Lord Denbigh looked sadly across the table at Marian. "Marian has done all she can to reign in the girl's poor manners and ill-breeding, but she has failed." Marian opened her mouth to interject but Lord Denbigh raised a hand to silence her. "That's not wholly your fault. But Miss Fuller's presence is undermining the purpose of our stay in Kent." He redirected to Mr. Fuller, pointing at him with his fork. "Send her home. Without her, there's no reason for Marian to stay so she'll go home as well. Then we can concentrate on our business."

Mr. Fuller seemed stunned, caught between the urge to argue and the wisdom of acquiescing to Lord Denbigh's demands. Fear coursed, cold and dark, through Marian's blood. She could imagine herself separated from Katherine and sent back to Warwick Paddox alone. Sorrow and loneliness struck her in the gut. That could not happen. Not when she had promised Katherine her heart.

Through her fear, she saw a chance in Mr. Fuller. He seemed as reluctant to send Katherine home in disgrace and unattended as Marian was to be separated from her. "Mr. Fuller," Marian spoke up brightly. "What is Miss Fuller's experience with the Continent?"

Mr. Fuller's brow creased. "Limited. She and I went to Paris last year for a few weeks but the war stopped travel to Europe for ladies of her age."

"Did she enjoy Paris? How was her behaviour there?" Marian prayed that he would either catch on and follow her lead, or that Katherine had miraculously been well behaved in France.

There was a brief flash of confusion on his face, which Lord Denbigh thankfully missed as he speared a sausage and brought it to his mouth, then Mr. Fuller seemed to follow Marian's thoughts. "She found Paris very agreeable. Katherine was very much at home there, and very well behaved."

That was enough of a concession for Marian to proceed with the rapidly forming plan in her mind. "If you are reluctant to send Miss Fuller home, you could send her to the Continent for a tour."

"I couldn't send her alone. I need to stay here to complete our dealings in England. She would need a chaperone." He had clearly caught on by now and was putting his support behind

Marian. She smiled at him across the table and saw a bit of Katherine's mischievousness smile back at her.

"I have not been to Europe since before the war as well. I could go with her, as a companion."

Lord Denbigh's head shot up at that. "Marian, you're not old or experienced enough to travel as the companion of a headstrong girl."

Marian had not had the proper time to consider this argument. She was unused to arguing against her father, much less in the heat of the moment. She floundered.

But Mr. Fuller was prepared to come to her aid. "Lady Marian and Katherine have spent quite a bit of time together and I have noticed Katherine's demeanor and manners quite improved after her time with Lady Marian." He gave Marian an encouraging smile.

It gave her enough strength to speak up again. "Yes, I am fond of Miss Fuller and believe I can make a positive change in her behaviour if given enough time."

Lord Denbigh looked between them, unconvinced. "Was her behaviour last night an example of this improvement? I don't see how-"

"Last night was an unfortunate set back," Marian cut in. "But we have been making real progress in improving Miss Fuller's manners and tact. I want to continue that. I think I can do more if we were to go to Paris."

Lord Denbigh shook his head and bit into a rasher of bacon. "I don't like it, Marian."

She took a deep breath, gathering her strength for a last push. "Father, I think the cultural exposure would do Miss Fuller a world of good. I know you, Henry, and Mr. Fuller have important work to do here to secure your business interests. Miss Fuller and I can leave you to that while we continue to improve her etiquette."

Marian dropped her voice and took up a more personal tone. "I think of Katherine very much like a sister. With Cecilia married now, I miss having someone to look after." She could see her father's resolve weakening. "Let us at least go to Paris while you finish your business. We don't have to do a grand tour of the Continent. Just Paris."

Lord Denbigh's mouth remained set in a hard line. "She told some very important people lies about our proposition. Lies told out of misunderstanding and ignorance, not malice, but damaging all the same. We need time to undo that damage."

Mr. Fuller used this small concession to Marian's argument to show his support again. "Your idea of sending Katherine away is a good one, my Lord. I am sure I could concentrate more fully on finishing our plans here if I knew Katherine were safe in Paris under Lady Marian's good care and attention." He paused and suddenly looked unsure. "I am reluctant to send her across the Atlantic alone."

Marian tried not to blush at that, remembering what kind of good care and attention she had been giving to Katherine lately.

"If it's the best way to guarantee our success here, Marian, you may travel to Paris for a few weeks with Miss Fuller." He gave his say-so with a sigh, as if he were granting some great boon.

It was all Marian could do not to jump out of her seat with joy. She and Katherine would be away from here, away from the weight of their ordinary lives, as soon as she could arrange it. They would live as themselves for a few weeks at least. She smiled at Mr. Fuller.

He smiled back and Marian began to question how much he might know about his daughter and her preferences. And how Marian fit into what he did know about Katherine. "I'll arrange for your passage and lodging in Paris, Lady Marian. Thank you for accompanying my daughter while your father and I finish our business here."

"You're welcome, Mr. Fuller." Marian was truly fighting a blush now. Mr. Fuller's gaze was piercing but not unkind. He was a much sharper man than his good nature made him seem. "I am sure Miss Fuller and I will have an excellent time in Paris and we can continue to improve her behaviour while we are there. I'll pass on the good news to Miss Fuller after breakfast."

Mr. Fuller nodded at her before tucking into his own breakfast in earnest. Lord Denbigh turned his attention firmly back to his papers. It was all Marian could do to remain in her seat and eat her breakfast at a leisurely pace. She wanted to race back to her room, catch Katherine still abed, and crawl in beside her to relay the news.

✿ ✿ ✿ ✿ ✿ ✿ ✿ ✿ ✿ ✿

When Marian returned to her room, almost *their* room now, Katherine wriggled in the bed, pulling herself more firmly under the covers and away from the light as Marian drew back the curtains.

"You've missed breakfast."

Katherine barely hummed an acknowledgment.

"You will have to go back to your own room at some point, you know." Marian pulled open another curtain to let in even more sunlight. She loved teasing Katherine like this. It made her feel comfortable and safe that she could poke and prod at Katherine without fear that Katherine would become angry or irritated.

Katherine did see fit to roust herself at that gentle chide. Her sleek brown bob was now a mass of tangles and impressed upon her face were lines from where she had cuddled into the sheets. "I'm lucky you're not kicking me out right now."

Marian couldn't bring herself to tease about that. Marian was happier than she had ever been in her life and wasn't about to let one night of heavy drinking and loose talk ruin that. Especially considering the news she had come to share.

Instead of teasing, she smiled serenely at Katherine and sat on the edge of the bed. Katherine immediately wrapped an arm around Marian's waist and pressed her face to the cotton of Marian's day dress where it covered her thigh. "It's good you missed breakfast. I ended up sharing the meal with both our fathers."

Katherine groaned. "How angry are they?"

Marian reached out and attempted to smooth down Katherine's wild mess of hair. She was only marginally successful but Katherine sighed and pushed her head up into Marian's hand, like an eager cat. She did not want to make her beloved wait long for this news but savouring the telling of it filled Marian with glee.

"My father is angry. Your father seems to think you're behaving rather better than usual."

"Ah, that's my solid old pater. Always there when a girl needs him to cover her ass."

Marian swatted at Katherine's bottom. "Language, Miss Fuller. I am to be teaching you lady like behaviour, remember?"

Katherine burrowed her face further into Marian's lap. "Yes, miss."

"Is that something he's done a lot then?"

Katherine peeked up from Marian's thigh with a wicked grin. "Once or twice. But no more. I am a reformed woman."

Marian stopped the slow strokes through Katherine's hair to tug lightly on the ends. "I don't believe that and neither do you."

The grin twisted into an unattractive grimace, morphing Katherine's normal dimples into sorrowful divots. "I will try, Marian. I promise."

She sounded so remorseful that Marian could not help but slip from the side of the bed and settle on her knees on the floor. They were at eye level now and Marian could easily grasp Katherine's hand. "I know you will. But I do not expect you to change completely, or right away. I don't even want you to change all that much. Just to have a bit more discretion."

Katherine looked dubious, her frown staying firmly in place. Marian added the only thing she knew would make Katherine smile: "I love you." It was an easy confession after the ups and downs of the last several hours. It had been unspoken between them, known but hidden.

Katherine's frown melted away until her lips ticked just a bit upwards at the corners. "I love you too. I'm very happy you put up with me."

"My father wanted you sent away. Back to New York, alone and in disgrace."

"What? No. No, my father wouldn't do that. He'd never allow it." Katherine shot straight up in bed. Marian rose with her and reclaimed her seat on the edge of the bed, leaning close.

"Shh. No, he didn't allow it." Marian curled her hand around Katherine's cheek to calm her. "Your father and I talked him out of it."

"Talked him out of it? You can talk your father out of the something like that?" Katherine was as amazed as she was confused.

Marian smiled. The news she had raced up here to give was about to bubbled over. The look on Katherine's face was going to be worth a thousand hard conversations with her father. Marian would take him on every day if it would make Katherine smile.

"In fact, we talked him into something better."

"That I can stay in England with you forever?"

"No, but maybe even better than that. Your father is arranging for us to travel to Paris for a few weeks while they finish their business here." Marian's face split into a wide smile as understanding dawned on Katherine.

She sat up even straighter in the bed. "But we'll need a chaperone."

Marian laughed out loud. This was the best part of the plan. The part that guaranteed them privacy on their trip. "I'm your chaperone. I argued, and your father agreed, that I am old and wise enough to keep my eye on someone as headstrong and willful as you are."

Katherine launched herself forward into Marian's arms. Her lips came down, hard and fast, against Marian's. The kiss was scorching, with lips and tongue sliding together to pull a groan from deep within Marian's chest. She melted against Katherine, giving herself over to this conquest of a kiss. One of Katherine's hands wrapped in her hair to tip her head back and expose her throat above the neck of her dress. Katherine's other hand cupped and squeezed around her breast. The feel of Katherine's palm rubbing across her nipple through the fabric was tantalising and made Marian ache for more.

"We are going to go to Paris and I am going to have you in a giant bed with the balcony windows thrown open so we can hear the city streets below." Katherine nipped at the cords in Marian's neck.

Marian stretched upward to give more of the delicate skin of her throat over to Katherine's mouth, arching her back to push her breast more firmly into Katherine's hand at the same time. The thought of making love so openly, still in a private room but with windows open and sunlight streaming in, frightened and excited her. France's social mores were different but they would still need to be discreet, surely? She let herself be pushed backward across the bed. Katherine quickly settled over her, held up by her elbows.

"Did you know there are women like us who gather in Paris? They're artists and writers and poets." Katherine bent her head and kissed her way along Marian's jaw. "Maybe we can find them."

"I'm pleased to hear we'll be leaving our hotel suite. I thought you might try to keep me there the entire time."

Katherine sucked lightly on Marian's throat, until Marian tried to wriggle away. "Not the entire time." Her eyes burned with desire as she rocked her hips against Marian's.

The curtains were open and they were only on the third floor. It was early in the morning and maids or other guests could be anywhere. It made Marian nervous. All thoughts of more open love making in Paris were pushed to the side.

"Kitty. We can't."

"Why not?" Katherine punctuated her point but working a thigh between Marian's legs and pressing down.

Marian arched up into that thigh, grinding against it even through layers of clothes, before she could stop herself. "You need to go back to your room and make it look like you spent the night there." Katherine snorted at that. "And I need to… speak to your father about our travel arrangements."

"Father can handle it. Unless you're going to tell him to book us one room instead of two, then I definitely support you leaving to speak with him."

Marian weighed that comment against how quickly Mr. Fuller had agreed to Marian chaperoning Katherine on this trip. "Does your father know about us? About this?"

Katherine placed one last kiss against Marian's jaw before sitting up away from Marian's supine form. She shrugged. "He may suspect. He knows at least some of what I got up to at school and in the New York social scene." She smiled wickedly as Marian pushed herself up from the bed. "At least the bits I got in trouble for."

It was unfathomable that a father could know these things, know what his daughter had done and what her inclinations were, and ever look upon her favourably again. Katherine and Mr. Fuller seemed to like and respect each other in a way Marian was unused to seeing between fathers and daughters.

"He knows about you and-" Marian waved between them with a frantic hand, "-what you do?"

Katherine shrugged as she stood. "He knows enough. It's not like I sat him down and explained some sort of sapphic birds and the bees to him." She let the borrowed nightdress fall to the ground and Marian was momentarily distracted by the line of her bare back and soft curve of her hips. Katherine picked her discarded undergarments and ball gown from the untidy pie on the floor where it had fallen the night before. She shimmied into her clothes while Marian watched, mouth gone dry with desire. The casual display Katherine was putting on stoked the fire their kissing had started earlier. It took great effort on Marian's part to pull herself back to the conversation at hand.

"It's remarkable that he still…"

"Still what?"

"Still includes you in family affairs." It seemed cruel even as she said it, but sons and daughters had been disowned for less.

Katherine moved to the side of the bed and presented her back for Marian to do up the buttons she couldn't reach. "That's love, I guess. It makes you overlook all sorts of unsavoury things."

She was so nonchalant about her father's continued acceptance. Marian could never imagine her own father being so accepting, much less deliberately sending his daughter and her lover to Paris for a respite from prying eyes. It was shocking.

"You do know how lucky you are, don't you? Most families, fathers or mothers or anyone else, would have tossed you out on your ear. They'd be so ashamed, they'd never speak to you again." Her voice was quiet and likely betrayed more of her own fears than her amazement at Katherine's situation.

As seemingly self-absorbed as Katherine could be, she was also incredibly perceptive. A trait that had taken Marian by surprise before, and would likely continue to do so. Katherine turned so that she was standing between Marian's knees. "We'll be very careful. Circumspect even. Your family won't find out. I promise."

It warmed Marian's heart that Katherine was willing to do this for her. "You can't make that promise. It's not entirely within your power."

Katherine bent and pecked a kiss to Marian's lips. "Watch me. I can do whatever I want and don't you forget it."

Any lingering fear and unease lifted and Marian laughed. "Of course you can. You always do."

"And now I can do it in Paris!" Katherine called out as the door to Marian's room swung shut behind her.

Chapter 15

Marian had spent years doing what felt like nothing with her days, waiting for something to happen to her. Now that she only had a few more days to wait to start a grand adventure, she was ready to crawl the walls with anxious boredom. She was only saved by a note from Cecilia inviting her to tea.

They walked through Cecilia's new gardens. Marian listened idly as Cecilia's explained all of her plans for the grounds. This was the kind of conversation Marian had expected to have with her sister after Cecilia married. Only she had expected to enjoy it.

Now, it was mind numbing. Marian didn't care about varieties of roses or what the Kent Ladies' Gardening Society might think about the fountains Cecilia planned to install. Whatever Cecilia planted would pale in comparison to the garden of sketched flowers Katherine was growing for her.

These were the mundane topics Marian had listened to her entire life and she was tired of them. Maybe she never cared about them at all. Her life was a polite facade, a lie told to more respectable women while her true nature simmered under the surface. Waiting for Katherine to bring it forward.

Now that it was out, this kind of life was nothing to Marian. She was filled with thoughts of Paris and adventures with Katherine. And love.

Roses just could not compare.

"But Father said you're going to Paris."

That comment, the first directed to Marian in a long time, caught her attention. "When did you speak to Father?"

It wasn't that Marian was avoiding answering Cecilia's question, but she was suddenly struck with fear that her sister, who knew her so well, would see through the veneer of friendship she and Katherine were hiding behind.

Cecilia continued, ignorant to Marian's fear. "I invited him to tea as well. He responded that he was busy and you likely would be as well, since you were now preparing for a trip to Paris."

It was such a direct answer and Cecilia was looking at her with such curiosity that Marian could not steer the conversation to safer ground. Her best strategy was to try to downplay the excitement she was feeling and hope Cecilia remained ignorant. "Oh yes, Mr. Fuller is arranging for Miss Fuller and I to travel to Paris while he and Father finish their business here. I expect it will be a relatively short trip. It's only something to keep us occupied while everyone else is busy. Just enough time to see how France is faring now that the war is over." Only a forceful snapping shut of her jaw stopped her babbling flow of words.

Cecilia looked at her oddly and Marian grew cold, scared that she'd given too much away. "You seem to have grown very fond of Miss Fuller since she came to England, haven't you?"

Marian tried to shrug nonchalantly but the motion felt stiff and wrong. "She's a nice girl. A bit headstrong but I like setting a good example for her. It's a challenge but she is trying."

"Her boisterous behaviour at the ball last night certainly did not recommend her." Cecilia gave a ladylike sniff before turning down another garden path. Marian hurried to follow. Cecilia might have been letting the subject drop, but Marian could not. The need to defend Katherine tugged at her.

"Yes, she was not on her best behaviour, but I spoke to her about it and made sure she got back to the hotel without incident.

She did not have the same sort of training and refinement we did growing up. She can't be expected to know all the rules." This strident a defence was probably treading on dangerous ground. Marian wasn't normally someone who argued strong opinions or stood up for others in the face of unkind gossip. Cecilia might reconsider how "very fond" Marian really was of Katherine.

Cecilia laughed. "Gracious Marian, I would think that any woman would know that giving your attention to so many men so enthusiastically is more than a bit uncouth. It doesn't take finishing school to know that."

"When did you become such a snob?" Marian snapped.

Cecilia stopped in the middle of the path. "I'm not a snob. You're much more forgiving of Miss Fuller's behaviour than you would be of anyone else. Even her lipstick is inappropriate! And you say nothing about it!"

Marian floundered. She wanted to respond, to set Cecilia down, but could think of nothing that wouldn't give her and Katherine away.

Cecilia laid a hand on her arm. "I'm just concerned that Miss Fuller is exerting more influence over you than you over her."

"You're the one who said I was lonely and that she would be good for me. That I needed a friend." Marian was equal parts angry and afraid of what Cecilia might suspect.

"That was before I realised-" Cecilia stopped, turned on her heel, and stalked away from Marian.

Marian followed a few steps behind Cecilia. The massive front door to Cecilia's new home was in sight. Marian's heart beat faster. Maybe they could make it back inside before Cecilia said anything else about Katherine.

Cecilia stopped her with a gentle hand on the crook of her elbow before ascending the stairs. "You could still marry, Marian. You don't have to resign yourself to... to that. You could have this too." Cecilia pulled her hand back in a sweeping motion to indicate the garden behind them and the house rising up in front of them.

Marian took a moment to look between the garden and the towering brick house, to take a deep breath of flower scented air. She would never have this. Even without Katherine coming into her life, this had never been in her future. She had never truly wanted it and felt nothing more than simple fondness for the boys she had known that had gone off to war. Katherine had only shone a light on what was already there.

"No, Cecilia," she said with a small smile. "I'm happy the way I am."

✵✵✵✵✵✵✵✵✵✵

She spent the hour before dinner hidden away in her room, with one of the hotel's ladies' maids, wrapping herself in her best dinner gown, twisting and pinning her hair, and applying creams and potions to her face. Lord Denbigh, Mr. Fuller, and Katherine would all be present this evening. Even with their agreement to go to Paris, the quiet family dinner had even odds of being cordial or going up like a powder keg put to match. Marian wanted her best armour. She would go to battle in satins and silks. If she was going to be completely disreputable behind closed doors, she would compensate by being the perfect image of propriety in public. That's what she had been trained for, after all. If the powder keg were going to blow, it would not burn her up along with the tablecloths and weaker souls. She would hold her own and shield Katherine as best she could. Paris wasn't that far away.

When she reached the large dining room, the footman directed her instead to the smaller private dining room which was set only for four. Marian was doubly glad she'd taken the time to properly coif her hair and pull on white gloves.

Lord Denbigh and Mr. Fuller entered the dining room on her heels. Mr. Fuller graciously seated Marian and poured her a healthy measure of wine before Katherine made it to supper. Katherine had adopted the same logic Marian had about the strength of an empowering frock. But Katherine's taste ran much more modern. Much too modern.

Her dress was short. Not shockingly so. Marian had seen other young ladies out at night with dresses that were shorter, but the hanging fringe of the black and silver sheath dress hung only just below Katherine's knees. The line of her stockings led perfectly down to shoes that were just a bit too high for polite company. Her hair was carefully arranged in pin curls around a black and silver headband with white and silver feathers standing tall. Her cheeks were rouged and her lips were red.

She was absolutely gorgeous.

Marian heard Lord Denbigh suck in an angry breath next to her but it was all she could do not to beam with pride. Katherine was stunning and strong and could not be put in her place. And she was Marian's. She wanted to be Marian's and no one else's.

Marian ducked her head and took a sip of her wine to cover the smile spreading across her face. The outfit wasn't inappropriate by current standards. It was definitely chosen to rile Lord Denbigh. Where Marian's inclination was to shrink and hide behind pleasant agreement until they could escape to Paris, Katherine's tactic was to face the gauntlet straight on. Both were shows of strength, in their way.

"Katherine, what a very modern dress. Is it new?" Mr. Fuller seemed nearly as mirthful as his daughter. His moustache twitched as he tried not to laugh.

Katherine gave a little spin and the tassels on her dress twirled around her legs. "Yes, I went into town and found a little dress shop quite overlooked by the ladies of Kent. They assured me this would be the height of fashion in Paris. I was able to pick it off the rack and have a few alterations made this afternoon." Lord Denbigh turned absolutely purple listening to Katherine's glee over her new outfit. "I have two more coming as soon as the seamstress can finish the changes." And with that, the vein in the middle of his forehead popped out as well. Marian felt no need to soothe him. Lord Denbigh could cling to his old ways but Marian would not make him feel secure there. It was time to embrace the new.

Mr. Fuller pulled out the chair next to Marian and gestured for Katherine to sit. She slid into the chair and smiled up at her father. "Do you really need three of these things just to go to Paris?" Mr. Fuller asked, not unkindly and with a twinge of humour in his voice.

"At least three. More if we were going to be away longer." Katherine was tipping over from 'cheeky' into 'mischievous' territory right before Marian's eyes. "I may have my entire wardrobe redone when we get back."

Mr. Fuller laughed at that and took his seat across from Katherine. "I would think you may want to keep a few longer dresses around. Just for the New York winters, you know."

"My knees will adapt."

"Or they may just freeze off."

The casual banter between the two was foreign to Marian. She would never talk to her own father this way. It wasn't just the level of informality, but the camaraderie as well that made it feel so intimate and different from Marian's own family experience. Considering that Mr. Fuller knew at least some of his daughter's less acceptable inclinations, maybe a little teasing about a dress wasn't so bad.

Marian stayed quiet, as did Lord Denbigh but with a distinct air of disapproval. She couldn't imagine that Mr. Fuller didn't realise that, considering how aware he was of what they thought had been secret goings on. He just didn't seem to mind. Not being bothered when others disapproved of Katherine was a skill Marian would need to learn in the near future. She imagined them together at a cafe in Paris with Katherine laughing too loudly or waving her arms too broadly as she related some tale. Marian would let the disapproving looks of the other imaginary patrons bounce right off of her. She wouldn't feel embarrassed or protective. She would focus on Katherine. Only on Katherine and how happy she was with Marian. Katherine was worth far more than just Marian's attention and respect, and she planned to prove that to her in Paris.

Or maybe the French wouldn't care at all.

Sitting quietly through the soup course was probably good practice for ignoring others' opinions of Katherine. The Fullers continued a light banter back and forth while Lord Denbigh seethed. As the soup dwindled, so did his anger. By the end of the roast beef and potatoes, Mr. Fuller and Lord Denbigh were discussing some other gentlemen they had met in Kent. It wasn't directly business talk, which would have been rude at the table in front of the ladies, but it was close enough that Lord Denbigh seemed soothed by it.

Katherine kept herself busy by idly picking at the chunks of potato left on her plate. She kept her fork in her right hand and rubbed the edge of her left thumb along Marian's knee. By now Marian was far too used to this behaviour to be shocked. And she certainly wasn't going to complain. She relaxed into it, pressed her knee closer to Katherine, and hoped that the length of the tablecloth would hide their movements from the staff who cleared their plates away.

Marian could scarcely remember what pudding was served because Katherine's hand was even more bold near the end of that course.

They were both brought back into the conversation by Mr. Fuller after the last of the plates were cleared away. Katherine pulled her hand away and Marian was sad to feel it go.

"If Katherine has dresses to be delivered, you two probably aren't interested in departing on the morning ferry, are you?" Mr. Fuller's eyes twinkled at Katherine and Marian's shocked faces. It was clear from where Katherine had inherited her impish streak.

"Tomorrow morning?" Katherine squeaked out while Marian snapped her hanging jaw shut.

"Could have been, if you didn't have dresses to wait on."

Marian could feel Katherine vibrating with excitement beside her. Katherine's hand shot out underneath the tablecloth to grip Marian's knee, this time with a forceful squeeze. "What if I went to the tailor's early in the morning to see if they are ready, then we caught the ferry just after lunch?"

Katherine beamed, caught up in the spirit of negotiation. Marian was too afraid to look at her own father. Did it seem scandalous to run off to the Continent just two days after Katherine's indiscreet behaviour at the ball?

Marian was about to speak up, to tactfully voice her concern about the speedy departure, but Mr. Fuller spoke first. "I imagine your tickets can be pushed back to the later ferry. I'll have to send a wire to the hotel to let them know you'll be checking in rather late. It will be a terrible inconvenience in the name of your dresses." Mr. Fuller rolled his eyes dramatically and rested the back of his hand against his forehead in parody of a swooning Victorian. Yes, he definitely contributed the impish streak to Katherine's personality.

This sort of play would never have been tolerated in the Fielding household. Katherine cackled in delight and rushed from Marian's side to hug her father. Lord Denbigh bristled at their exuberance.

"Marian, are you prepared to leave tomorrow? On either ferry?" Lord Denbigh's tone was bland but it was a deliberate jab aimed at Mr. Fuller for rushing them to Paris and not conferring with Marian before making arrangements.

She regained her composure and wiped away the ghost of a smile with the back of her napkin. "Yes, Father. I can ask the hotel staff to help pack my steamer tonight. I'll be ready for the ferry in the morning."

"Good girl. Now, Fuller, let's leave the ladies to the salon and get a drink." Lord Denbigh rose from the table and departed without a backwards glance. Marian was quite used to that.

Mr. Fuller made to follow Lord Denbigh from the room, and Katherine and Marian followed him to the door. Instead of leading them through it, Mr. Fuller turned and placed a gentle hand on Marian's arm.

"Thank you, Lady Marian, for being willing to take care of my daughter. Everyone needs someone to care for them." All his previous mirth had disappeared, replaced by deep sincerity and gratitude.

Marian was taken aback and unsure how to respond, or if she should respond at all, to such an unexpected display of genuine feeling. Katherine stood next to her, beaming with pride and happiness at her father. She leaned up to place a peck of a kiss against his cheek. Katherine turned to Marian, just a subtle shift of her shoulders, but it was enough to pull Marian out of her shock and paste a polite smile on her face.

"Of course, Mr. Fuller. I'm happy to accompany Miss Fuller to Paris and see that she has a wonderful trip." Deep in her heart, she could feel the pull to say more. To be less formal with these two people, one of whom she loved very much and the other who could end up being a close confidant, but years of training and good breeding forced her back into the role of a lady.

Katherine bumped shoulders with her father. "That's as enthusiastic a response as you're likely to get from Marian. She's still too British and genteel for great shows of emotion." Her tone wasn't patronising or belittling, but was warm and joyous instead. When Marian met her eyes, Katherine gazed at her with obvious love and affection. That caused Marian's cheeks to heat, both from want and from embarrassment that Katherine was making eyes at her in front of Mr. Fuller. But it felt lovely to be understood all the same.

Mr. Fuller gave a great, dramatic put-upon sigh. "Don't worry, my dear. I'm sure you'll have that beaten out of her in no time." He held the door wide and Katherine retreated to the hallway with a laugh.

Marian made to follow but Mr. Fuller stopped her with the gentle touch of fingertips against her sleeve. "Don't forget to make her take care of you too, all right? She'll need reminding about that."

She was still in awe of the kindness he extended toward his daughter, but to extend the same to the daughter of a business associate, a practical stranger, made Marian stop and look more closely at him. Even if he knew what Katherine and Marian were to each other, he barely knew Marian. The lines around his eyes spoke of someone who both laughed often and took on heavy burdens, but the dark sea blue of his gaze was so similar to Katherine's that Marian's fondness for him could only grow.

"I will, Mr. Fuller. I'll make sure we're both well taken care of."

Chapter 16

They made the early afternoon ferry, with Katherine's dresses in a carefully wrapped brown paper package, but only just. They had taken a car to the dress shop and from there directly to the ferry at Dover. Katherine stood at the rail and let the sea splash tiny flecks of foam on her cheeks as they pulled away from the pier, pure glee shining on her face. The sun beat down and caught strands of auburn in her dark hair. How could Marian still be caught off guard by her loveliness? It took her breath away.

Mr. Fuller had booked them a small cabin for the journey. Katherine would have been happy to spend the entire crossing on deck, letting the sun add freckles to the bridge of her nose, but Marian managed to coax her below so they could rest and have tea. The pitching of the ship made Marian's stomach roll. Never enough to be sick, but enough to be uncomfortable. Being lower felt more stable and the heaves not as great. Sitting on a cushioned bench was much more comfortable than watching the Channel churn and bubble as it was sucked beneath the ship.

The tea was weak but serviceable. The carefully cut sandwiches were less appealing, but their late evening arrival in Calais meant little else would be available, so Marian forced some into her unsettled stomach. Before long, they transitioned from boat to train, and Marian slumped, exhausted, against Katherine in the privacy of their first class car. Katherine locked the door, pulled the shade, and wrapped an arm around Marian's shoulders.

It was still odd to be so openly intimate with Katherine. Marian's shoulders stiffened as she rested her head against Katherine's chest. The fear of discovery stayed with her, deep in her gut like a lead weight, but the sound of Katherine's heartbeat against her ear soon soothed her. Her muscles relaxed, spine curled and eyes drifting closed. The rhythms around her — Katherine's heart, the rocking of the train, and the sweep of Katherine's hand down her back — lulled Marian to an uneasy sleep. She didn't open her eyes again until the train slowed just outside Paris.

"Did you stay awake all this time?" Marian asked as she rubbed sleepily at her eyes, a gesture she tried not to indulge in, sure that it would make her look younger and childish. But with only Katherine to see and the shroud of sleep still clinging to her mind, it was impossible to resist.

Katherine smiled back at her as Marian pulled away, feeling rumpled and travel-worn. "Mostly. I think I dozed a bit."

"I hope I didn't dribble on you."

"You wouldn't dare. Not even in sleep."

It was more Katherine's nature to be overly optimistic than it was Marian's, but she felt her heart grow light and buoyant in her chest at Katherine's smile. And at the way Katherine's fingers curled against her palm.

The station, the motorcar to the hotel, and the ornate lobby passed in a blur. Katherine pushed her along by force of will until they were ensconced in a suite of rooms which had two bedrooms, each with a ridiculously overlarge and overstuffed bed, connected by a sitting room. Each bedroom had a small water closet crowded by a large porcelain tub. There was a cold supper waiting for them in the sitting room.

Marian watched as the porter deposited her trunk at the foot of the bed and gave the man thanks for his late night assistance. She could hear Katherine banging drawers and shuffling about in her own room while she laid out her dresses. At least, she hoped that was what Katherine was doing. They had declined Lord Denbigh's offer of hiring a maid and informed the hotel such service would be unnecessary as well. Privacy on this trip was of pinnacle importance to both of them.

Regardless of their desire to be truly together and themselves as much as possible, Katherine had opened a new world of self-sufficiency and independence to Marian's eyes. The world was changing and Marian wanted to be able to properly take care of herself. She could air out a dress and hang it herself while only delaying her supper a few moments. If Katherine was going to have daring dresses made, Marian could order some that she could easily put on and take off herself. The idea filled her with independent pride.

Katherine was apparently much faster at unpacking, or perhaps just lost interest somewhere in the process. She strolled into Marian's room, chewing on a piece of bread and slice of cheese. She threw herself back on Marian's bed and continued to chew.

"You realise I won't be using my bed at all. That room is a glorified wardrobe while I'm here."

Marian smiled and folded away the rest of her intimates before turning to face Katherine. She was slowly sinking into the fluff of the feather duvet and piles of pillows. "And what if I decide to sleep in your bed instead?"

Katherine rolled to the side and propped her head up enough to see Marian over the duvet. "You won't. Because no one is going to come wake us in the morning."

Marian had been thinking about that since they had declined the presence of a maid. For the entirety of their trip to Paris, she could fall asleep in Katherine's arms and wake up the same way. No one would disturb them. Even if they were discovered, it would be far less scandalous here than in England.

Lord Denbigh might not even find out. Seeing Katherine reclining among the pure white fluff of the four poster bed, and knowing that no one would come for them, made Marian's cheeks heat and her stomach clench with desire.

Supper could be skipped. She'd make up for it at breakfast tomorrow.

✿✿✿✿✿✿✿✿✿✿

Marian almost missed breakfast as well. She was sound asleep, wrapped with the plush covers against her bare skin, until Katherine threw back the curtains, pressed a kiss to her brow, and handed her a warm croissant and cup of coffee.

"We're being very Continental now, *ma cherie*," Katherine drawled in a terrible French accent.

Marian was still too tired and travel-sore to complain.

"I'll draw a bath." With another kiss to the forehead, even though Marian had tipped her face toward her for more, Katherine was gone. The luxury of a hot tap in the bathroom sounded wonderful. A long, hot bath to relax her muscles and refresh her spirit was exactly what she needed.

She pulled a dressing gown from the armoire and wrapped it around herself before slipping into the bathroom. Katherine was bent over the tub, her dress stretched over her backside in a way that was both enticing and a little scandalous. From the lack of lines and shadow, Marian could see she wore nothing underneath. Katherine flipped the taps off and tested the water with her hand before stepping back and waving Marian forward.

Marian let the robe fall at the side of the tub. Being so shameless in front of Katherine, in the well lit and open bathroom, still took a considerable amount of courage. The thought of her body being something that should be hidden from Katherine was slipping away with each night they were able to spend together. By the end of this trip, Marian might just forget herself and take Katherine over a bench in a public park. She snorted an unladylike laugh as the water closed over her body. Really, Katherine would like that far too much.

She rested there for a few moments, breasts buoyant and peaking just above the water line and head resting against the cool porcelain, before she felt Katherine tap her shoulder. Marian opened her eyes to see Katherine standing above her, hands on hips and gloriously nude.

"Budge up."

Katherine had also opened the doors to the balcony just across the room from the tub. Marian sat up in shock.

"What are you doing?" She pulled her knees up to cover herself.

"I'm climbing in. Slide up. I'm getting in behind you."

Marian obeyed but kept her eyes on the open doors. "I meant the balcony." She hadn't expected Katherine to join her, but it was the less disreputable of the two issues presenting themselves. Well, maybe not less disreputable, but certainly less unexpected.

Katherine slid in behind Marian, legs spreading so that her knees knocked against Marian's thighs. With hands on shoulders, she urged Marian to lean back and rest against her chest.

"I wanted to enjoy the view," Katherine nodded toward the open doors, "while I enjoy the view," she ran a hand down Marian's bare side under the water.

Marian groaned. "You're terrible." But it was a lovely view of the city rooftops. The sun was warm and the breeze was fresh.

"Relax," Katherine kissed the shell of Marian's ear. "No one can see. I wouldn't put you in danger like that."

Marian believed her. She knew that Katherine would never mean to hurt her or put the two of them in danger, but she also knew that sometimes Katherine did things without thinking of all that could go wrong. But that was the consequence of the impetuous nature that Marian loved so much.

She settled back against Katherine's chest, letting her muscles relax in the warm water. She had to slide quite far down to rest her head against Katherine's shoulder.

"Wouldn't this work better if I was behind you?"

"Why?"

"I'm taller."

Katherine kissed the side of her neck. "But I like it better back here." Her hands traced down Marian's side and her arms locked around Marian's ribs. Katherine took up a slow, up and down slide of her fingertips from just under the curve of Marian's breast all the way down to tickle the edge of the fine blonde curls between her legs. Katherine kept the touch light, never drifting to her breast or sex directly, in a way designed to drive Marian wild.

Marian pressed her backside more firmly against Katherine. She arched her hips, rolled her shoulders so that the taut peaks of her nipples crested the water. But all with no response from Katherine.

She was ready to give up. To concede defeat and admit that this was all a game that would lead to no greater pleasure. There was a touch of unladylike petulance in her voice when she spoke again.

"You could at least wash my hair while you're back there."

Katherine's fingers kept to their path, but this time her thumb just barely grazed the underside of Marian's breast before sweeping down again. That flesh, that had tingled with the desire to be touched for the long minutes Marian had been at Katherine's mercy, sparked hot with lust.

Katherine hushed her. Her fingers reached the end of their downward sweep and dipped just an inch lower to scratch through Marian's curls. Marian's hips jumped up in response, making a little splash in the tub, before Katherine hushed her again. "I'm busy right now, but maybe after."

Oh, *after*. After was good. It meant something was going to happen first.

Marian tried to move her hips again, a slow circle this time instead of a thrust upward. Katherine's hands pushed back and held her steady. "I didn't think you were going to do anything." The petulance was still there, but now overlaid with hopeful anticipation.

Katherine kissed the shell of Marian's ear. Her breath tickled, warm and moist, against Marian's cheek. "I'll do anything you want. You just have to ask me for it." Marian couldn't see Katherine but she could feel the curve of Katherine's lips still against her ear.

Marian bucked her hips up again, taking Katherine by surprise. Katherine's fingers slipped just a bit lower but did not quite reach Marian's center. She tried again, this time rolling her hips back and forth. Marian couldn't keep a small gasp from slipping out when Katherine's fingers began to move with her. Katherine mimicked the stroking Marian wanted to feel, just not in the right place. The pads of Katherine's fingers smoothed her curls but did not part her flesh. It was maddening.

"You have to ask with words." Katherine's voice had dropped as she spoke against Marian's ear. Katherine's teeth nipped gently and Marian felt Katherine's hips rock against her backside. Marian smiled, knowing that Katherine wasn't unaffected. It made her want more.

She could have pushed Katherine into action with nothing more than the wanton tilt of her hips and a well timed moan. She knew how close to giving in Katherine was. Marian could tell by each press of Katherine's breasts to her back and each slide of Katherine's hips against her bottom. But what was so hard about asking for what she wanted? Why did the behaviour feel less shameful than putting the desire into words?

Maybe it was a learned skill. Something she just needed to practice.

Marian tilted her head back and twisted her neck to kiss Katherine's lips. She was off balance and her neck strained but Katherine devoured her. Marian felt the slick heat of Katherine's tongue against her teeth as Katherine thrust into her mouth. She tried to reach around, to grasp at Katherine any way she could, but Katherine held her still with a firm hand on her hip.

Katherine's stroking fingers stalled their movement as she pulled away. "Sweet Jesus, Marian. Please…"

Katherine was begging. Pleading with Marian to take them this one step further.

"I want you to use your hands on me. Rub your fingers and palm against my sex. Push into me until I find release."

It sounded, and felt, awkward coming from Marian's mouth. The words were stilted and inadequate to explain how much she needed it.

Marian gave herself over to Katherine's care. She pressed her face against Katherine's neck as Katherine's fingers finally found her center. Katherine stroked, and plucked, and pushed until Marian's hips were rocking up hard enough to splash water over the edge of the tub in an attempt to grind against Katherine's palm and force Katherine's fingers more deeply inside her.

"Come on, my love. My dearest." Katherine's fingers thrust faster, pulling out until just the tips remained inside Marian's body then pushing back in with some force, as she rubbed the heel of her hand against that sensitive nub at Marian's center. Marian sobbed. "I want to watch you fall apart."

Marian bent her arm at the elbow to hook it behind Katherine's head. She grasped Katherine's shoulder and the new position gave her more leverage to thrust up onto Katherine's fingers. She pushed against the restraining hand Katherine kept on her hip. Marian arched her back up, forcing the small swell of her breasts from the cooling water. "Kitty," she whined.

"You have to ask, remember?"

This time, the words came much more easily. "Touch my breasts. Grab them and squeeze. Please."

Katherine was quick to use her free hand to comply. This left no restriction against the movement of Marian's hips. She rolled them forward to get closer to Katherine's hand and pushed her chest higher in counterpoint to the thrust of her hips.

"What else?" Katherine's hips had stilled against Marian's bottom. Her voice was tight with control.

"Pinch my nipple between your fingers. Hard. Pull on it." Marian tried to hide more firmly in the crook of Katherine's neck to cover the blush growing across her face.

"No, darling." Katherine butted against the top of Marian's head with her chin. "Don't hide. Look here." She nodded toward the open balcony doors and Marian's gaze followed hers. "Look at this beautiful city. It's our city now. It will always be our city, where we can be together and be ourselves." Katherine's fingers pushed deep and stayed there, letting Marian grind against her. "I am going to make love to you as much as I can while we're here. I want you delirious with lust so all you remember when you think of Paris is pleasure."

Marian moaned and her limbs began to shake. She was reaching her peak. She could feel it coiling hot and low in her belly. She wanted to tell Katherine, to ask for something more or just to warn her, but her breath would not become words. Her eyes were locked on the Paris roof-line and all she could do was cry out in Katherine's arms.

Katherine knew how to read the signs of Marian's body. Her fingers thrust in and out while the heel of her hand pressed hard against Marian's center. The hand grasping Marian's breast slid upward to pinch the tight point of her nipple. Katherine grasped it hard, twisting and pulling. Katherine was saying something, some words of love and desire, against Marian's temple but Marian could not hear her. Her ears roared with the sound of sea waves and darkness blurred the edges of her vision. All her muscles went taut at once, and hung there for just a moment too long to be comfortable, before letting go in a great rush of overwhelming pleasure.

She didn't faint. Not exactly. But it felt as if she were floating both within the cool water and somehow above it. Marian was aware of Katherine easing out of the tub and gently lowering her so her head rested on the porcelain rim but her muscles were too weak to assist.

The view of Katherine's legs, water running down their length and dripping from the soaked tangle of dark curls between them, soon blocked Marian's view of the open balcony doors. Katherine climbed back into the tub and Marian feebly pushed herself up, muscles shaking, expecting Katherine to settle against her chest in a reversal of their earlier position. Instead, Katherine did not settle, just stood over Marian.

Katherine bent her knees and rubbed at her own sex directly in front of Marian's face. Fingers parted her curls and folds to flick across the nub at her center. She watched Katherine rub and roll across that nub for a few beats before looking up into her eyes.

"Marian-" was all Katherine managed before Marian wrapped weakened arms around Katherine's thighs to pull her forward.

"Here. Kitty, come here." Marian's murmurs were quickly muffled against Katherine's skin. Marian slid down against the back of the tub and Katherine bent her knees against the rim near Marian's ears. The position let Marian work her tongue over Katherine's folds, to flick against her center, and twist into her opening all while Marian rested her head on the cold porcelain and gazed up the long line of Katherine's naked body.

Katherine rocked her hips, grinding herself against Marian's mouth. It was almost too forceful but Katherine's desperation only made Marian grasp more firmly at her hips. Marian tugged Katherine's hips to encourage her to writhe against Marian's lips and tongue.

"This won't take much longer," Katherine gasped out. The muscles in her thighs jumped and twitched and Marian moved to soothe them with her palms. It was both a disappointment and a relief to hear that Katherine would not be pressing against Marian's face for long, using Marian to seek her own pleasure in such a single-minded way. The thought of lying back and letting Katherine take what she would from Marian, of providing pleasure and of being lovingly used, sent a little shock of wanton glee down Marian's spine.

The roll of Katherine's hips grew faster and the grind of her sex against Marian's tongue harder. Marian watched as she raised both hands to pluck at her nipples, just as hard but much more quickly than she had done to Marian. Her stomach quivered and her knees shook. Marian could taste a hot, fresh rush of Katherine's wetness across her tongue as Katherine cried out above her.

She pitched forward, catching herself on the edge of the tub with outstretched hands and bowing her back to keep her sex against Marian's lips. Marian surged up, locking her arms around Katherine's hips and flicking her tongue across her center, until Katherine's cries fell to whimpers and she pulled away.

Marian lay for a moment in the now cold water, lips tingling and sticky, gazing up at Katherine and her wobbly knees. Katherine gazed back with a beautiful, and dumbfounded, smile on her face.

"God, you are so beautiful," Katherine said. Instead of stepping from the tub as Marian expected, Katherine slide back down into the water, her front pressed to Marian's, and covered Marian's face with kisses. The porcelain was even colder than the bathwater and hard against her back, but Marian stroked Katherine's flushed skin and kissed her in return.

The sounds of the city soon intruded from the streets below. Katherine drained the tub and refilled it with hot water. This time she did wash Marian's hair.

Epilogue

August 1924

The bang and clatter of metal pots assaulted Marian as soon as she opened the front door. She balanced her parcels between her hip and the wall to have a free hand to lock the door behind her. It was a habit that had been hard to set in stone. That first year, she was always leaving the door of their tiny London flat unlocked. They had been in a decent part of town back then, not as nice as their neighbourhood now, but it still had been a dangerous oversight. Her family always cautioned her that two young women living alone needed to be careful. Even Katherine took that to heart in those early days.

And it was Katherine who must be responsible, at this very moment, for the racket coming from the tiny kitchen tucked at the back of the flat.

The opportunity to sneak up on her was too good to be wasted. Marian eased her parcels to the hallway floor, trying to keep the brown paper wrapping from crinkling too loudly. Not that Katherine could hear it over whatever she was getting up to in the kitchen, but it seemed like the thing to do when trying to sneak up on someone.

Marian made it all the way down the long hallway to the kitchen doorway before Katherine's antics shocked a laugh out of her. Her beloved was standing in the kitchen, apron tied sloppily over a pair of brown trousers and plain white button down blouse, with what appeared to be every pot and pan they owned pushed onto the overcrowded hob. The huff of laughter that escaped Marian had Katherine spinning in place, with a messy pot raised to her chest.

"Marian!" Katherine's mouth pulled into a perfect "O" of surprise. Her hair was shorter than when they'd met, and straightened every morning by hot curlers to tame the wild waves into a sleek bob. By evening, if Marian curled a piece around her fingers, it would bounce back into the shape she loved. "You're home earlier than I thought!"

"Not early enough. What are you doing?"

Katherine lowered the pot to the equally messy worktop. "I'm making you a celebratory dinner."

Marian raised the courage to take a few steps closer to Katherine's mess, inching her way to the stove top. "Were you?" She peered into the pots bubbling with questionable-looking liquids. One seemed to be nothing more than water brought to a rolling boil. "You never cook." It was the most diplomatic way she could think to point out there was a reason Katherine never prepared their meals. Marian's skills at diplomacy had only grown in the years living with Katherine. As had her culinary skills.

"I know. But it's celebratory." The exasperation in Katherine's voice made her sound very young and Marian couldn't help but smile.

She leaned back against the worktop, careful not to rest against anything that would leave a stain. "What are we celebrating with-" she waved at the simmering hob "-this."

Katherine brightened immediately. "Daddy has gotten a very good offer on some of his American railway holdings."

Marian tried to stay abreast of the Fullers' business dealings, especially those Katherine was involved with, but it still sounded like gibberish to her. She had learned as much as she could about investment and trade while Katherine had served as a behind the scenes adviser to her father, but it was never enough to hold a reasonable conversation. During her girlhood, she had feared becoming a wife to a businessman consumed by his work and she had ended up in a strange parody of that fear anyway. And it was wonderful.

"That's very good. So he's going to sell?" This was as far as Marian's business knowledge would take her.

"Yes, and he's going to reinvest his earnings." Katherine smiled broadly and Marian recognised it as a pause for suspense. "With me."

Katherine beamed, obviously overcome with joy. Marian smiled back at her but did not fully understand.

"That's wonderful. But what does that mean, exactly?" Marian kept the smile on her face in an attempt to cover her ignorance. Katherine had no business interests of her own, nothing substantial to invest or invest in.

Katherine rolled her eyes, not unkindly, and came forward to kiss Marian lightly on the tip of her nose. "It means that Daddy is going to let me take the money he makes from his railway interests and redistribute that to our work here. Investments and business interests that he's going to let me oversee. I'll have much more responsibility. I won't just be his eyes and ears while he's out of the country. I will have my own interests to take care of." She grew quiet. "It will be like I'm running my own businesses, Marian. Think of it!"

Marian's smile had only grown as she watched Katherine's animation at the idea of Mr. Fuller increasing her responsibility in their family business. She might not understand the reasons why Katherine and Mr. Fuller got so excited about certain prospects, but she could appreciate that excitement when she saw it.

"That's wonderful. Definitely a night for celebrating then." She looked back into the questionable pots. "What are we celebrating with?"

Katherine bit her lip and joined Marian in peering into the pot. "It was supposed to be a pasta bolognese."

"Why do you need six pots and a frying pan for pasta bolognese?"

Katherine's brow furrowed as she gazed at the overflowing hob. "I don't think I did. Well, one was because I burned the sauce the first time and had to start over."

Marian looped her arms around Katherine's waist from behind. She rested her chin on the crown of Katherine's head. It was a position of intimacy and comfort that Marian often took with Katherine.

She pressed a kiss to Katherine's ear. "I brought cabbage and fresh sausage from the market. Do you think we can salvage this or should we have those?"

Katherine sighed. "I wanted to make you something to celebrate."

"We can still celebrate." Marian turned Katherine in her arms so they were facing each other. "I'm very proud of you. You're going to be running all of your father's affairs one day."

"That's what men without sons will have to start doing. Especially if their daughters aren't going to give them sons-in-law or grandsons to take over." Katherine shrugged off Marian's compliment but Marian could see she was pleased. Katherine snuggled more tightly into her arms and kissed the hollow of her throat where the soft, worn cotton of her dress dipped low. "Maybe someday I can keep you in the comfort you deserve. Rich estates and servants again."

Marian tipped Katherine's chin up and brought their lips together. It was a slow, searing kiss. The kind Marian never would have initiated in their early days but now it was the most natural thing in the world. She dipped into Katherine's mouth and trailed wet heat across Katherine's tongue and teeth until Katherine moaned in pleasure.

Marian pulled back. "That's nonsense. I am exactly where I want to be. This is a much better life than I ever hoped for." She slide her hands down Katherine's back to cup her bottom, lifting Katherine slightly to give her a fleeting press of lips to lips. "Besides, I couldn't kiss you in the kitchen if we had servants."

Katherine laughed against her lips. "If we employed the right kind of servants, you could."

"I don't think 'do you enjoy the poetry of Sappho?' is a regular question one asks when interviewing housekeepers."

Katherine laughed again, this time against Marian's throat where she pressed tiny, open mouthed kisses. "But we could. We could do anything we want."

Marian squeezed Katherine's backside and drew her up a little higher, intentionally rubbing their breasts together through the fabric of their clothes. "What I want is to eat a simple dinner of greens, maybe a sausage, and whatever we can save from your turn at cooking and then to take you to bed. That's enough celebration for me."

"Yes," Katherine kissed her again. "Yes, my love, that's all we need."

About the Author

Gretchen Evans is a married, bisexual, cis woman living in North Carolina. Her day job involves figuring out the best way to ask people questions they don't want to answer. In the evenings, she does hot yoga and watches any TV show that can be read as queer-coded. She only drinks beer disguised as root beer and her perfect Sunday involves half-listening to an NFL game as she reads a book. Though she has been writing fan fiction for more than a decade, How to Talk to Nice English Girls is her first original work. She plans to continue writing queer romance with engaging characters, sexy times, and feelings.

About Carnation Books

Carnation Books is a fandom-powered publisher of the best in inclusive fiction. Founded in 2016, Carnation Books is at the forefront of new author discovery. Visit CarntionBooks.com to learn more, and to sign up for our story-filled newsletter!

CPSIA information can be obtained
at www.ICGtesting.com
Printed in the USA
FSHW012004041020
74461FS

9 781948 272094